Enjoy the read and
never stop dreaming.

Sharyn Jaeger

About the author

Sharyn Jaeger was born in Scottsdale, Arizona, and attended
Arizona State University, where she later earned a Master's
degree in Criminal Justice.
In 2008 she moved to the beautiful coast of California, and
now calls Santa Barbara home.
Sharyn is an animal lover who has rescued five dogs and
continues in efforts to stop animal cruelty.

This book is dedicated to anyone that has ever chased a dream. If you don't like your story, write your own.

Sharyn Jaeger

DEADLY CLIMAX

AUSTIN MACAULEY
PUBLISHERS LTD.

A CIP catalogue record for this title is available from the British Library.

ISBN 9781785546655 (Paperback)

www.austinmacauley.com

First Published (2015)
Austin Macauley Publishers Ltd.
25 Canada Square
Canary Wharf
London
E14 5LQ

Printed and bound in Great Britain

The importance of this book is to allow for someone to escape their reality and become connected with the characters that have been created in this book, and to feel a passion or thrill that may be missing in one's life.

Prologue

Sex, sex, sex, you could do it all the time, yet it never seems to be enough. It has always been one of America's favorite pastimes. A man could be down to his last penny and if he had to choose between a meal or a roll in the hay, you could guarantee that in the end, that man would starve. It is a recession-proof business. Sex is a need, a want, a desire. It's used as a weapon, a tool, and a way of life. It had been a way of life for Lucy Lust for the past five years.

Lucy Lust, of course, was not her given name, but that of a persona in which she had created; a persona in which she is selling fantasy, fetish, and desire to those who are incapable of creating it for themselves. She wasn't your everyday streetwalker. She had earned herself some very established customers. She was pushing 31 years old, but could easily pull off 25 in her business attire. Tonight, it was a small black satin skirt that was just long enough to accentuate her perfectly round ass, but short enough to show off her long legs, accompanied by a blue lace shirt that was laced just tightly enough to accentuate her small, but perky b-cup breasts and shadow her perfectly hard nipples.

She looked at the calendar and shuddered as she saw that it was only three days away from the end of 2019. Even in the harsh December winter in New York, the pricks would be out, looking for entertainment for the pricks in their pants. She decided it was too cold for her open-toed shoes and opted for black lace stockings and her thigh-high black leather boots. She often changed the complete look of her persona by switching up her eye color, hair color, and style of dress, in order to keep her clients from getting bored. Tonight's eye color was a mixture of all of them, giving her eyes the illusion of a rainbow. She chose these contacts to match her perfectly frosted eye shadow. She glanced out the window and decided it was too cold outside for short hair, and after some debating, put on her long brown-haired wig. Although it wasn't real hair, it was long and thick, and it tickled her back where it laid on her bare skin. She did one twirl in front of the mirror, and decided she looked damn good tonight.

"And the night begins. Time to freeze my ass off and pretend to like these pervs so I can pay my bills," she said to the mirror as she took one last glance and headed out the door of the small studio she rented.

As soon as she walked outside, she was assaulted by the teeth-clenching cold and the little flakes of snow that had begun to fall. Instantly, her nipples were hard enough to cut glass. She was contemplating just saying "screw it" and heading back inside, but then she remembered the long black dress in the Barney's storefront window that had her name on it. It was a Rick Owens Grecian Gown and only $3,450. She was halfway towards having enough money for that dress, and if her night went well, she would be heading to Barney's by the end of the week. With her goals in sight once again, she walked the three blocks to her favorite spot and screwed on her fake, sexy smile and got to work.

Prostitution was still illegal, but the law tended to look the other way. Since 2015, when all the licensed companion laws were put on the bill, people had different views towards prostitution. None of the bills passed, leaving sex-selling illegal, but it seemed to not be worth an officer's time to deal with it. So, Lucy was not surprised anymore when a John walked right up to her on the street with cash out in hand, not being the least bit shy.

Her first John of the night was an early bird. It was shortly after 10:00 pm, and he came staggering up with a cheeky grin on his extremely round face.

"Hey cupcake, it's my birthday. Wanna give me a present?" He sloshed out, in between burps.

It's everyone's birthday when they want free sex. Lucy responded, "I will tell you what, since it's your birthday, how about you tell me what you want and I will pretend extra hard to like you and smile the whole time."

"Okay cupcake. You have a deal. I have $50 and a car parked down the street. I promise I will smile the whole time too. It's my birthday."

Fifteen minutes later, Lucy was $50.00 closer to her gown and extremely happy she hadn't been vomited on. She told the guy he shouldn't drive and helped him call a cab home. She left him as he was telling the cab driver for the third time that it was his birthday, and she headed back to her spot.

Two hours and three Johns later, Lucy was $500 richer and ready to call it a night, when she looked up to see a sinfully handsome man walking her way. He was tall, very well built, and had a face that could have only been designed by God himself. *No way this guy needs to pay to get his rocks off*, she thought to herself. As he walked right up to her and smiled with his very sensual lips, she found herself thinking about how good it would feel for her lips to caress his and realized this one would be business AND pleasure. He grabbed her hand and brought it gently to his lips and lightly brushed them across her hand. This caused her thighs to start throbbing as he blew his hot breath against her hand and said, "Good evening, beautiful."

"It is evening, but I don't know about the good part. I am freezing my ass off out here," she said, not trying to sound rude, but this was the first time she was tongue-tied.

"I have a hotel on this street if you would like to get out of the cold. It would be my pleasure to spend some time and money with you. My name is-"

"I don't do names," she said abruptly, cutting him off. This had always been a rule for her. They were all just John, but she didn't know if she believed herself this time, as she found herself wondering what name went with his perfectly chiseled face. "I find that it is easier to keep yourself anonymous with certain business dealings. I go by Lucy Lust, but for the right price you can call me whatever you want."

"I will just call you beautiful, if that will please you", as he outstretched his arm, linked it to hers and escorted them down the icy street to his hotel.

When they reached the hotel she saw that it was the Millennium Hilton Hotel and had to hold back a little whimper of joy. She wasn't sure if she was more excited about the hotel or to get out of the damn freezing cold weather. She was fairly sure that she stopped feeling her ass a couple hours earlier. She wasn't at all surprised that he wanted to enter through the garage, as her attire was far too flashy for this hotel's upscale lobby. Then again, that was her intention in wearing such attire. They continued to make their way in and took the elevator to the 18th floor. They headed down the long, luxurious hallway. He stopped at room 1810 and unlocked it with his key card. They stepped in and the door closed with a loud thud behind her. The room was large, with modern art and furniture. There was a black leather, odd-shaped couch in the center of the room with a glass tabletop made up of shattered glass pieces joined together. Everything she looked at seemed to be a piece of art. There was even a full-size kitchen filled with artistic knick-knacks. The theme seemed to be black and cold steel, but it worked.

Lucy turned to look at the deadly handsome man offering her a glass of champagne. She took the glass and took a small sip. She had been in the business long enough to know if something had been slipped in it. One small sip and she could tell if the taste was off. Satisfied with the taste, she took a bigger sip, felt the bubbles travel down her throat and smiled. "Now that the pleasantries are done with, shall we discuss price," she asked him with a flirtatious grin.

He pulled out two $500 bills and set them on the counter. "Here is what I have. What I want is pleasure, excitement, and highly erotic. Can you provide me with all that?"

"I can provide you with all that and much, much more," she said as she unzipped her skirt and felt the smooth satin caress her hips and legs as it fell all the way to the floor. She stood there, standing in her black lace thong that barely covered her moneymaker that was there between her soft thighs.

He walked over to her, grabbed her hair just enough to pull her head back and expose her neck. He seductively brushed his lips over her neck before teasingly nibbling her ear. His eyes met her eyes, and he watched as her pupils dilated while he ran his fingers over the top part of her lace panties. She could feel her heart beginning to beat rapidly as he slowly slid her panties to the side and used his fingers to explore the heat inside her. Before he took her over the edge, he stopped and asked her to take the remainder of her clothes off. She happily obliged his demand and stood in the middle of the living room, letting him enjoy the view. He simply smiled and got down on his knees in front of her and began to explore her again, but this time with his mouth. He used his tongue to drive her rapidly over the edge. As she came for him, he simply smiled. He picked her up and took her to the bedroom. When he dropped her on the bed, she could see that he was hard as a rock and almost exploding out of his jeans. He stripped himself naked, exposing a perfectly sculpted body. He reached his hand out for hers and brought her up to him. She knew exactly what he wanted and brought him as close to climax as he would allow with her skilled mouth.

"Roll over," he said as he pulled her head back by her hair. She did as she was told and he pulled her hair to the side to expose her naked back and the temporary butterfly tattoo she had put on that night. He gently skimmed his hand down her spine to the nape of her butt. He was not gentle when he began to take her. He moved with speed as he rammed himself into her. It didn't hurt, it felt good, but she was surprised at the mood change. He grabbed a fist full of her hair as he moved in and out of her. She felt her breath catching and unable to stifle the screams of pleasure as he took her over the edge once more. They came together and he released himself on her bare butt.

He collapsed next to her on the bed, trying to catch his breath. Looking at him was like looking at a god. He was glimmering from all the sweat and she noticed that he was still very hard. She was pretty sure she could hear her own heartbeat in the silence of the room. As if almost reading her mind, he got up and turned some music on and climbed on top of her. He began thrusting inside her again and placed both hands around her neck.

His hands were a little too big and a little too tight for her liking. "I don't do that," she said as she tried to remove his hands from her neck, but they only tightened. Unable to speak or give commands to him anymore, she started to panic. She was fighting for air and beginning to see stars. She couldn't focus, but she was trained and knew how to get out of these kinds of situations. She had enough know-how to take care of herself. The panic set in and she couldn't quite remember the training. Instead, she flailed and flung her legs until he lost his balance just enough to loosen his grip a bit and for her to get off the bed. She got up quickly, but not quick enough, as the fist intended for her face slammed into her shoulder. Her shoulder exploded with pain and she felt him grab for her hair. He pulled the wig off in one forceful tug, and managed to get a chunk of her real hair too. Pain was swimming through her head as she tried to focus.

"Get over here you stupid little cunt," he shouted. "I paid for fun, pleasure, and excitement. You promised me all three and you can bet I am going to get them all from you. You are about to find out what I call a good time."

She tried to run out the room, but he grabbed her by the waist from behind and flung her on the bed with such force that she almost bounced off. She grabbed the only thing she could get her hands on and flung it at his face. The glass vase shattered against his chest and he looked at her and gave her a devilish smile. He came at her and she made one last attempt for the door, but was crushed to the floor with his body. As his hands closed around her neck again, she reached for a piece of the broken vase and stabbed him with it. He screamed out in pain

7

and tried to pull the piece of glass from his neck. Lucy was no longer coherent in what she was doing as she grabbed another piece of the broken vase and repeatedly stabbed him in the throat and chest. When she realized that he had stopped moving, she stood up, looked down at the blood everywhere, and ran into the bathroom. She became nauseous, as she looked in the mirror at all the blood covering her naked body.

Lucy walked into the room and stared at the man she had just killed. Self-defense or not, there was no way she was going to admit to killing a man. She went through the hotel room and erased any sign of her being there. She wiped surfaces where fingerprints could be, wiped her bodily fluids off his, and put her champagne glass in her purse. She was not going to let this asshole win and ruin her life. She put on a hotel robe and a shower cap to cover her hair and prepared to leave. She stopped once more to look at the man who still in death remained nameless to her. She caught herself smiling and realized her heart was pounding not from fear, but from exhilaration. She told herself it was just from coming so close to dying. But, as she walked out of the room and took one more glance back, she realized it was because she had enjoyed killing that asshole.

Chapter 1

Sarah Carmichael stared out the window at the snow that had begun to fall. It was 6 o'clock in the morning and her shift didn't start for another two hours, but she was awake as always. Along with the snow, the morning brought on an excruciating migraine. She could feel it at the base of her skull and she was tense all over.

"Babe, don't you ever sleep? I love to sleep at your place, but I am always waking up alone." Wesley Porter, her longtime boyfriend, looked at her with a sleepy smile as he patted the bed for her to come back and join him.

Sarah sauntered over and looked into his gorgeous blue eyes and ran her fingers through his perfect brown head of hair. She loved the way it felt between her fingers. "Not all of us are lucky enough to wake up looking as good as the Prince of New York City. I have to get up and get ready for work. I don't roll out of bed looking all sexy like you do."

"You know I hate it when you call me Prince, darling. My father is only the Mayor. You can call me Prince when he becomes Governor," he laughed out as she scowled at him. "And I must say, you do look pretty damn sexy this morning. Actually, good enough to eat," he said as he grabbed a handful of her shiny chin-length blonde hair. He kissed her passionately on the mouth while she tried to let out words of protest.

"Wes, I have to get ready for work," she giggled out in between kisses.

"I love it when you play hard to get Lieutenant. I promise you that the crimes are not going anywhere. If it makes you feel better, you can restrain me and read me my rights. You do know how I love to be a bad boy for you," he said as he pinned her arms above her head and restrained her instead. He sat above her and stared into her crystal blue eyes. He knew from experience how cold and intent those eyes could be, but this morning they were playful and flirtatious. He leaned in and began to slowly kiss her neck, then moved his way down to her breasts. She shivered with enjoyment as tingling chills danced up and down her body. He firmly cupped her breast in his hand while gently caressing her nipple with his tongue. She whimpered out each time he would take a small nibble, leaving her breathless. His hand slowly made its way to part her smooth, long legs, but she anticipated that and opened without any effort on his part. Her body was aching, ready to receive his long, lanky fingers, but instead he made his way down with his mouth. She arched her back as the first stroke of his tongue caressed her. After a few minutes, she could stand it no longer and begged him to enter her. He obliged to the demand and climbed on top of her. As he slid himself inside, she realized she was holding her breath and let out a small whimper of delight. He clasped his hand inside of hers above her head to gain leverage and with that, she felt him with such strength she knew it would only be a matter of time before she climaxed.

Sex was a good way to start the morning, Sarah thought, as she listened to the quick beating of Wes' heart. They lay tangled in each other, shiny from the sweat shared and both trying to catch their breath. The moment was so peaceful until Sarah's phone started playing the specific ringtone she had set for dispatch. That ringtone meant her morning, and someone's life had just been interrupted by murder. Death was her job and she was more than aware that it had no respect for the time of day or special moments that want to be left undisturbed. Already knowing what was coming, she answered her phone, "Lieutenant Carmichael."

Thirty minutes later she was standing in front of the Millennium Hilton Hotel, watching her partner walk out. Amy Jones was twenty-six years old and full of life. She lived for the job and had just made detective three months prior. Even out of uniform, she pressed her pants, shined her shoes and always wore her vibrant, long red hair pulled back in a tight ponytail. She had a sullen look on her face as she approached and gave her the update, "The victim was discovered by the room attendants at around 6:40 this morning, when he missed three wakeup calls. No one touched the body or anything in the room and the first on scene has ensured no one entered the room until you arrived. It is room 1810 if you–"

"–Have you checked with the front desk to see who was registered to that room, Detective?"

"Yes, ma'am," Amy said as she looked down at her notes. "The name registered with the front desk is Adam Wright. They copied his ID at check-in and provided us with a copy. From what I have heard, once the blood is cleaned up we should be able to use the picture to ID him. I hear it is a mess up there. Lieutenant? Are you okay this morning?"

"I am fine, just fighting a nasty migraine," she said as she rubbed her hand along the spot on her head that was throbbing. She grabbed the ID from Amy and stared at the man known as Adam Wright. "Let's get up there and check things out before the crime scene techs show up."

She walked through the extravagant lobby and pressed the button for the 18th floor. As she walked towards room 1810 she saw the officer on duty come to attention. She walked in past him and took in the sight of the living room. It was large and surprisingly quiet. She made note of the open bottle of champagne on the counter and the single glass next to it. "No obvious signs of a struggle in this room. Looks like all the action was in the bedroom," she said as she turned and headed into the master bedroom. She could smell the death in the air and the blood that was soaking through the carpet. There, in the middle of the room was a naked and what once appeared to be, a very handsome man, lying on the floor covered in blood. There were pieces of glass all over the room. It was easy to tell what piece of the glass had been used to kill him, as it was still sticking out of his chest.

Noticing Sarah's glances at the broken shards all over the room, Amy said, "According to the manager, these pieces all over the room once made up a very expensive vase. Most rooms in the hotel have a decorative vase on the office nook in the master bedrooms, which is also where I found his wallet and verified his ID with his license and credit cards, but I will make sure his prints get run. Looks like hitting him with it wasn't enough for the guy who did this."

"What makes you assume it was a man? Is there any evidence in the room that leads you to that conclusion Detective?"

"No ma'am. I assumed by looking at the size of this guy. He has to be 6'3" or 6'4" and easily pushing 250 pounds with all that muscle. I had just assumed a woman wouldn't have been able to take him down." At the steely glance from Sarah, she continued. "I know better than to assume anything. Sorry Lieutenant. You taught me better than that." Looking up at the noise level from the other room, she carefully moved around the body and said, "The techs are here. Better get out of their way and see if they can get any prints or other DNA."

"Find out if the front desk knows if he was here for business or pleasure. Let's get a look at security discs and see what Mr. Wright was up to while he was here. Find out if he came and went with anybody during his stay. Let's also get a look at his personal history. I want to know if he has a criminal history, his medical history, his finances, his family and friends. Get me it all. I want to know who this guy is and who had a reason to want him dead. I'll be in my office when you get any information."

"Yes Lieutenant. Right away."

Three hours later, Sarah was assaulted by a full-blown migraine while she was finishing a report on her most current closed case to pass on to the commander. She was ready to move on to Adam Wright as Amy knocked on her door. "Tell me we have something useful, Detective."

"I am afraid at this point we don't. Mr. Adam Wright was 35 years old, single, no children and lived here in New York. He owned a fairly successful construction business. I have forensic accountants going through his financials now, but nothing has popped up so far. He only has one prior from when he was 21. It's a domestic violence charge. According to the reports, his fist met with his then girlfriend's face because he had found out she was diddling his best friend while he went to work each day."

Before continuing, Amy decided to rest her feet and sat down in the chair across from Sarah. "According to the manager, Mr. Wright checked in yesterday evening around 6pm. That is eight hours prior to the time of death established by the medical examiner. He checked in alone, ordered a steak dinner and a bottle of champagne to his room at 8pm. The room attendant was greeted at the door by Mr. Wright and says he did not see or hear anyone else in the room, but that Mr. Wright requested two glasses for the champagne. A Miss Lydia Florence saw him exit the hotel alone at 11pm, but there is no one who can confirm when he returned. The key card to the room puts him entering at 12:47am. From what the crime scene techs told me, the place had been completely wiped clean. No prints anywhere, except for what appear to be Mr. Wright's on the champagne bottle and glass. They are assuming all the blood is his, as it is all A-positive. DNA will confirm, but that takes time. The security cameras just happened to malfunction last night and the discs have been corrupted. There are no usable visuals." Amy paused for comment, but in Sarah's silence she continued, "But, like always, I saved the best for last. I knew that would perk you up," she said in response to Sarah's eyes widening a bit. "They did find a couple hairs. They were synthetic and brown in color. Most likely they're from a wig. The techs are working on getting the manufacturer. I was thinking we should look at streetwalkers or call girls. Maybe one of their "business managers" or a jealous boyfriend got angry. Seems to me whoever did this is smart and knows their way around security; maybe a little out of a hooker's league in terms of capabilities and expertise. But I guess it's a place to start."

"You are half right. Whoever did this is smart, but don't count out what those girls on the street are capable of. Times are rough. Some of those women were lawyers and even preschool teachers once. Let's not count them

14

out yet. I am more inclined to go with a pissed off pimp or boyfriend. Maybe this guy got a little too rough and our girl called in back up. It's hard to say at this point with absolutely nothing to go off of. I am heading out to meet Wes for lunch. Keep digging."

"You are so lucky. You know how many girls fantasize about Wesley J Porter? It should be a crime how pretty he is," Amy gushed.

"Amy, you may be my friend, but I am still your Lieutenant. If you ever call my boyfriend *pretty* again, I am going to put you on traffic duty for a week."

"Yes ma'am, sorry ma'am," Amy said giggling. "You enjoy your lunch; I am going to go fantasize about someone who is definitely not Wesley J Porter."

"Better not be doing that on the clock. Take a break and then get me something I can use on this Wright case," she said smiling and heading to the garage where her car was parked.

Chapter 2

It was midday and of course the streets of New York were jammed with people. As always, she was late to have lunch with Wes. She was starving, but she was not looking forward to the discussion regarding the New Year's party at his parents' house. Not only did she hate getting dressed up, but she wasn't a fan of hanging around his father, Richard Porter, the Mayor of New York. His mother, Virginia Porter, was no peach either. Neither, Richard or Virginia tried to hide the fact that they didn't approve of their golden boy, Wesley, dating a New York cop who didn't fit their breeding standards. She parked down the street because she refused to pay for valet and sighed to herself. *Why did Wes always insist on eating in restaurants with valet and annoyingly bubbly hostesses that always made her feel underdressed?*

She walked the one block to Nobu New York and used her fingers to comb out her hair. She made sure her badge was showing, hoping to keep the hostess from bugging her. She walked in, blew past the hostess stand and spotted Wes sitting at a table. It was obvious by the look on his face that she was a little more than five minutes late like she had thought. "I know, I know, I am always late. Yes I have a watch and a clock on my phone. I don't want to hear it Wes."

"Well, it's nice to see you too, darling. I can tell you have had a rough morning so I will forgive you," he said, rising to kiss her on the cheek. "And being so damn cute gets you some points too. I ordered for you. Got you the usual, the chicken teriyaki donburi."

"I appreciate it, but I really don't know why you always have to pick such fancy places. Can't we ever just meet up at a burger shack or something?"

"Oh yes, because eating a burger from a shack sounds delicious. You know I love their Salmon Tartar. And what's wrong with wanting to spoil my favorite girl?" he asked with a cute little smirk.

"You weren't even trying to hide the ass-kissing that time. What's up Wes? Why did we need to meet for lunch today? I'm in the middle of a new murder investigation."

"My mother," he put his hand up to stop her from interrupting him, "wants to know if you have purchased your gown for the New Year's party and would love to know who the designer is."

"I know she hates the way I dress, but I don't need a fashion coordinator; especially your mother. We have been together for six years, I am well aware of how to appease Virginia Porter by now."

"She has never said she hates the way you dress. She is just very excited about this party. You know how she loves to host big shindigs like this."

"The first event I went to with you she stared at me like I was wearing a sign that said I bought my dress at a thrift store." Ignoring his attempts to stifle back a laugh, she continued. "I swear, sometimes I think you only date me to irritate your parents."

"Sarah, you know how much I love it when you sulk and pout. My big bad Lieutenant worried about what my mother thinks of her. It's too cute. I recall last week sometime, you told me that you had found a dress

17

already. At Barneys, right? I know my mother, anything from Barneys will do."

"It's a little out of my price range, so it has taken longer than I thought to save for it." Knowing the look on his face, she cut him off, "No, you are not buying the dress for me. I don't care what occasion or anniversary you make up in your head to validate it as a gift. The answer is no. I am actually going to buy it tonight after my shift. That is if no one else happens to get murdered." At the same time, the waiter set their food down, with a judging look on his face. Apparently, murder was not an appropriate conversation piece for a table at Nobu New York, she thought while mentally rolling her eyes.

The meal put Sarah in a better mood and she was ready to get back to work. Wes grabbed her hand and brought it to his lips. He kissed her gently and said, "It was lovely as always. I'll be working late tonight. My father wants me to go over the budget again. I won't be able to make it by tonight, but you better plan on modeling that new dress for me tomorrow."

Remembering she had to go shopping, she started to pout. "Is it weird that I am a woman who finds the thought of shopping excruciatingly painful?"

"Not at all. It is one of the reasons I adore you so. You are so uniquely you. That, and dating you irritates my parents," he smiled and winked at her.

"I knew it! I have to get back to work. I am going to go question a few of the street girls. And no before you ask, you cannot come with me. I need something on this case. I am not even sure which direction to start in."

"You'll get your man, Lieutenant. You always do." He leaned in, kissed her and gave her butt a quick slap as she walked away.

It had been three hours since she left Wes and she was still putting off shopping. Instead, she called Amy to find out if there were any leads on the Adam Wright case. When Amy answered, Sarah already knew the answer. "How is it possible that nobody saw him enter the hotel with anyone? Or that the techs came up empty as well?" Amy was rarely irritated, but it was oozing out in her tone. Did you have any luck talking to any of the streetwalkers, Lieutenant?"

"No. Nobody within the five blocks I went down remembered seeing him or a girl with a long brown colored wig. From what I heard, most of the girls like to get creative and don't do the modest brown. I got absolutely nowhere. Call it a day, Jones. Go home and get some rest. Nothing else we can do today."

"Affirmative. I need some rest. You looked tired today. You better get some rest yourself."

Does needing rest supersede needing a stupid party gown? Though the thought of shopping had the migraine coming back, she headed to Barneys. The only positive thought in her head was that at least she already knew which dress she was getting.

The streets were packed and Sarah felt as though she was just another sardine shoved into the already overly crowded pouch. It was against her better judgement, and she rarely did it, but she flipped the lights on her cruiser. It didn't help much because there was already nowhere for anyone to go, but eventually people managed to move to the side. To think, all that, and it only saved her roughly eight minutes of her precious time. At least that is what she told herself. She justified using her lights because she honestly felt as if it was better than her impatience making her explode like a firecracker. She loved New York with such a passion. Even the smog and

19

the immense amount of rude, angry people running around couldn't make her change her mind. This place had always been her home and always would be. She just wasn't feeling very loving toward it today and knew it was not going to take much for her to snap. So again, she reassured herself, it's for the good of others, that's why she could use her badge for her own gain. She chuckled to herself in response to her logic, pulled up to the curb as close to Barneys as she could get, and threw the car into park. She wasn't ignoring the very large red and white "No Parking" sign, she just told herself it was speaking to everyone else today and that for her, it need not apply. She was sure the sign maker did not want to be responsible for her going ballistic on someone. She climbed out of the car and made sure her badge and gun were showing on her hip as she strode through the lavish front doors of Barneys.

As soon as she walked in, Sarah was hounded by a bouncy blonde. She couldn't help but notice her lips were about three sizes too big for her face. Sarah quickly asked for the dress she wanted, and it was as simple as that. The purchase had, of course, emptied her savings, but it was worth it to give Virginia Porter one less thing to sneer at her about. Quick and painless, she thought. She continued to tell herself that, yet the tightening in her chest didn't seem to relax until she was about halfway home. Unlike the other cops in her division, she chose to live fifteen minutes outside the city. She enjoyed the quiet and didn't mind the drive. Her street seemed to always be calm and the trees made it feel like she had left New York and went somewhere new each day she drove home. It was simple and it was hers. She pulled into the driveway, leaving room for her to get her personal vehicle out if needed. Leaving her department-issued cruiser in the driveway was done as a statement.

She knew it made her neighbors feel safe and it scared the miscreants who might think about screwing with her house. It didn't happen often in this neighborhood, but like on every street with families and pre-teens, the occasional drive by egging or toilet papering was known to occur. Thinking of how happy she was to have never had her house egged or toilet papered, she got out of her car with a smile. Just another perk of having the badge, she grinned.

Unlocking her front door, she walked inside and finally the last bit of tension in her chest surrendered and she let out a long, deep sigh of relief. She loved her small, comfortable living room. She found it to be inviting. Her mother would call it quaint and homely. She wasn't sure what her father would have called it, as she had never met him. She found it annoying to think about a man so often, when he really had no impact on who she was or what she had accomplished in life. She brushed the thought of the man she had never known, out of her head, and went back to thoughts of her mother. It had been nearly four years since her death, but Sarah still thought about her everyday. The cancer had come on very quickly and then spread rapidly. When she thought of her mother, she always wished she had more time with her, but in the end, she was grateful it was quick and mostly painless.

Missing Wes, now she began to wish that he was there to take her into his arms and bring her comfort, but she knew better. If he said he would be working late, he meant it. It pretty much meant he would be working into the wee hours of the morning and she would be lucky to see him by dawn. He hadn't even been working late the night before and yet he still hadn't managed to get to her bed until after two o'clock in the morning. She knew his job was demanding and that budgets would keep him up and away from her all night and maybe even the next day. With her thoughts all over the place, Sarah drew the curtains on her windows and sat down on her smooth brown suede couch to relax for a moment. Her shift may have ended, but her day had not, she told herself, resting her head on one of her many throw pillows. She knew she had things to do, but a quick nap wouldn't hurt. She closed her eyes and took a nice deep breath.

Chapter 3

Lucy Lust was back on the clock and back on the streets. It was 11pm and cold outside, as usual. It was later than her normal start time, but it had taken some persuading on her part to go out and get to work. She needed the money, but the previous night's events had made her a little leery. She recalled all the blood in the hotel room and it had given her a rush she couldn't quite explain, and wasn't ready to accept. She had just stepped out of the studio apartment she rented, where she kept all of her work wear. It wasn't a home, but it was her own space where she could freely be Lucy Lust. Not only did the tiny, dingy studio hold all of her attire, but it also held all of her secrets. This studio and the street were the only places Lucy Lust was allowed to run free.

She didn't spend much time there, so it didn't bother her that there was nearly no furniture or décor. She had a futon, a closet, and a vanity with all her wigs and makeup. It was all Lucy Lust needed. Tonight she didn't want to be flashy or stand out. Low key and out of the spotlight was the best option for this evening. Just make a couple hundred bucks and call it a night, was the goal. She stood on the icy sidewalk, staring into a storefront window, at her reflection. Images of the previous night's misdeeds flashed in her mind like a movie reel forcing her eyes shut as she shook the images from her head. "Damn it Lucy, what's done is done," she said aloud to herself in the reflection. "Tonight is a new night, you've got to let it go." She still was trying to figure out if the thoughts disturbed her or excited her.

With that thought, she made one last adjustment to the short, dark brown-haired wig that she had chosen. This one required her to have her own hair pulled back tight and pinned into place. The wig was cropped and edgy, and it fell perfectly around her slim face. She chose brown for her contacts, and also for her eye shadow. Subtle was the look she was going for, but she had opted for fake eyelashes and classic pink lip gloss. After all, she did need to get noticed on some level, if she was going to make any money. Tonight's attire was black leather pants and a sweater that showed off a great amount of her cleavage. Tonight she was a great deal more ample than usual, due to the purchase of a wonderful new push-up bra. The blue sweater rested just above her waistline to show off a little tease of her perfectly flat stomach, and the arch right above her butt. The tall, black stiletto heels she decided to wear, would work fine since she had only planned to work a couple of hours or a couple John's, whichever happened first. The reflection in the storefront window was not her own, but that of what she created; it was Lucy Lust. She decided she was ready to go to another block, as this one was getting zero traffic. She took one last full-length look in the window, and walked down the street in the frigid New York night.

As she continued her stride, she thought about turning around and just calling it a night. She wasn't convinced freezing to death was worth the little bit of money she might make. As the mental battle was raging in her head, a car pulled up beside her.

"You looking to make some money tonight, darling?"

She cringed a little at being called darling, but walked over to the passenger window. When she bent down to look in the car, she was surprised to see an old man. His kind voice didn't match his old and worn face. She wasn't sure if the car or the driver was older. "What did you have in mind?"

"I just want something quick and simple. You play with you, I play with me. That's all I want for now, but if I become so inclined, may I touch you?" he asked sheepishly.

"It costs more to touch me, but let's see where the mood takes you. You got a room somewhere or you just want it in your car?"

"I can't afford a room and you. I know a quiet lot we can park in though."

"I don't normally do quiet parking lots, but you look harmless enough," she said and got in the car. Her actual thoughts were that he looked half dead and that he didn't have the strength to try and fight her. She wasn't even sure if he had the strength to jerk it. But that wasn't her place, and he was going to pay her, so what the hell. They drove about five minutes and parked on the backside of a park. It was quiet and actually peaceful she thought. At least it would be peaceful until the decrepit old man beside her was going to play with himself.

"Will you put your hair in pigtails for me and can I call you Tiffany?" he asked.

"You can call me whatever you want," she said as she put her hair in short pigtails.

"I would like you to take your shirt off and put your pants around your ankles, "he told her as he unzipped his pants.

Lucy obliged and removed her shirt to show off her breasts under her black lace bra. She slid her pants down to her ankles, exposing her matching black lace thong.

You could barely see her naked skin underneath, but she knew he saw it as she saw him get hard as he caressed himself. She hoped he only wanted her to touch herself, as he originally stated. She figured it would take too much of his fleeting energy to get himself off. *Better get this going and get it over with,* she thought to herself.

She slowly caressed her breasts and slid her hand down her belly. Slowly, she slipped her hand beneath her panties. As she did this, he grabbed her hand and moved it slowly over her thighs.

He stopped just for a moment and grabbed two of her fingers. "Show me how you please yourself Tiffany," he said as he slid her own fingers inside of her. As she moved in and out with her fingers, she began to moan and he moved his hand faster around his manhood. As he stared at her fingers intently moving in and out, he began to grunt and groan. "I am so close. You make me feel so good. I can't wait to be back inside of you Tiffany. I want to cum. Call out my name, call me grandpa."

At this, Lucy abruptly stopped. "Are you serious? Is Tiffany your granddaughter?"

"Hey, you get paid to do what I want, not to judge me. I am about to blow my load sweetheart and I am going to do it thinking about my granddaughter. So if you want to get paid, stop looking at me like that and get those pretty little fingers back to work."

She could feel the rage and disgust growing inside her. It started in the pit of her stomach and made its way up to her head. She felt as if the disgust was blinding and choking her. She could feel nothing but the rage. Before the old man even knew it was coming, she had her sweater wrapped around his neck. She had the arms to the sweater in her hands and pulled so hard that he came over the middle console. He was flailing all around the car gasping for air. She could see that his wrinkled, pathetic dick had gone flaccid now. All she could think about was that disgusting thing near his poor granddaughter. He kept fighting for air and trying to get his hand under the sweater, but in the angle she had him in, it would be impossible. At this point, he had to know he was going to die. A few seconds later, the fight in him was gone. His hands fell into his lap and his head fell to the side. He would never be able to use that pathetic thing on anyone else ever again. She shoved him into the sitting position and stared out the car windows.

"What the hell just happened?" she said aloud to herself. She looked over at the old man's lifeless body and tried to fight off the adrenaline so she could think clearly. She pulled her pants up, and quickly grabbed her sweater from around his neck. With some hesitation, she put it back on. She quickly removed the belt he was wearing and placed it around his neck and the other part around the headrest adjuster. She grabbed both of his hands and used them to scratch at the belt and then dropped them and let them lie where they fell. She found a rag in the backseat and used it to wipe away any prints she may have left. She wiped down the inside of the car and the outside for good measure. She walked around to the driver's side of the car and looked in the window. It looked like a clear case of auto erotica gone very wrong. She was satisfied with the staging and walked away. The world is a better place without a scumbag like that, was what she kept telling herself as she walked back in the direction of her studio. Halfway from home, she caught herself smiling. At that moment, she decided it was time to call it a night.

Chapter 4

Sarah awoke on her couch the next morning, in the exact spot she had fallen into after work. She felt surprisingly rested for five o'clock in the morning. She stood up, stretched, and opened the blinds to find out the sun had not yet begun to rise up. There was still leftover snow on the ground from the previous night. It shimmered and sparkled as it melted beneath her porch light.

It was going to be a cold morning, but at least she had time for a quick, hot shower and a cup of coffee at home. Walking through the living room and entering her bedroom, she saw her new dress in its plastic wrap and shuddered. She almost forgot that she had to attend Wes' parents' New Year's Eve party tonight. She loved Wes, but god, she hated mingling with the type of people his parents invited to their ridiculously over extravagant parties.

Feeling a little grumpy now, she stripped down and stepped into the shower. Within seconds, the bathroom was filled with steam from the piping hot water she let run down her back. Wes always complained that she made her showers too hot, but she loved to feel the water relax her down to the bone. She stood for several minutes, just letting the water flow through her hair and roll over her bare back, thinking about the days past and the days ahead. She wasn't sure if she was more stressed about the current murder investigation she was conducting or the damn party she had to attend. Work comes first, she thought. Let's at least get through the day before I worry about tonight, she told herself.

She got out of the shower and opted for a robe while she let her hair air-dry and made a pot of coffee. Enjoying her favorite dark roast blend, she decided to enable her video chat to wake up Amy. As soon as her face appeared on the other side of the screen, Sarah knew she had accomplished just that. Amy's eyes were still half-closed, as she attempted to produce words that weren't slurred from sleep.

"Well, how nice to get a wakeup call from you Lieutenant, is everything alright?"

"Good morning Amy. Yes, everything is fine. I just want to get an early start today. Adam Wright's cousin will be coming into the morgue today to identify his body. From there, I want to head over to his office and interview his secretary and see if we can find out any more about his lifestyle. Plus, I will be pulling you off shift early today. You are my miracle worker and I need you for tonight."

"From the look of your hair this morning, I would say you need nothing short of a miracle," Amy replied with a giggle.

"Hey, you don't look so hot yourself at the moment, Detective."

"I was rudely awoken just five minutes ago, what's your excuse?"

"Traffic duty is looking better and better for you each day," Sarah joked as she politely held up her middle finger for Amy to see. "Meet me at the station in an hour. I want to get this day started," *and over with very quickly,* she hoped. She cut off the transmission just as she saw Amy begin to roll her eyes.

In her bedroom, Sarah chose her usual pair of faded blue jeans and black boots. She was contemplating which top to wear, when she heard her phone beep, alerting her to a new email. She picked it up and smiled when she saw it was short blurb from Wes that read, "I missed you last night and I am thinking of you today. Love you babe." She smiled and thought how he had perfect timing. She was just trying to figure out what small, natural disaster she could arouse to avoid the New Year's Eve party. Reading the message, she remembered that she did it for him, so she would suck it up, and let Amy transform her into the perfect little socialite they all wanted to see. *Those are the things you do for love....right?*

Going back to the closet, she picked a simple black button-up shirt. She finished it off with her weapon harness and badge. She walked out of the bedroom, looked at the dress from Barney's and said, "It's you and me sweetheart, be ready for me because I need tonight to go well." Feeling confident and ready for the day, she headed out the door, got in her cruiser and headed towards work.

At the station, she sat in her office, waiting for Amy. It was nothing spectacular, but like her home, it was hers. Her chair had molded to her butt perfectly and her desk had its own perfectly organized mess that was all hers. She loved the noises and conversations she got to hear coming in from outside of her office. The cop talk and obscenities from the bullpen always made her smile. It reminded her of why she first joined the academy. The camaraderie and support cops had for each other was something that rivaled a true family. She was barely listening when she heard a bit of a conversation that perked her ears up. The words auto-erotic asphyxiation tended to get most people's attention. All she heard about the conversation was that some old man had died in his car, trying to please himself and strangled himself at the same time. The conversation was interrupted when Amy walked in. Apparently, she thought these guys needed a large box of donuts, as she set down some jelly-filled goodness for the guys to fight over. She winked at Sarah and smiled, "Men are so easily pleased," she said, proud of herself. "Geez, is that all it takes? A little auto-erotic asphyxiation and some donuts and they're like little kids on a playground" Sarah chuckled.

Before Amy even made it through her office door, Sarah said, "You are five minutes late Detective."

Smiling, Amy replied, "Yeah, but look how happy all the guys are. I did that. I love being the reason that many men are happy."

"Well, now that we have your daily bullpen ass-kissing out of the way, what do you say we go meet our current victim's cousin?" Looking at her notes, Sarah continued, "Her name is Vicki Donovan. She is the cousin of Adam Wright, on his father's side. According to the notes, she was the only family member willing to come claim his body. She drove over from Trenton, New Jersey."

"On paper, this guy doesn't sound so great. His own family doesn't even seem to give a rat's ass. I wonder if the room attendant hadn't found his body, if anyone would miss him."

"I don't care who misses him or not, that's not the least bit important. I just want to know who would want him dead, what he was doing in that hotel room, and what kind of guy he was. That will help us find out why he died." She grabbed a file from her desk, and brushed past Amy in the doorway. On her way through the bullpen, Sarah grabbed the last jelly-filled donut.

"Thanks Amy," she said with a wink as they headed out the office to the morgue.

When they arrived and walked through the doors, Sarah remembered why she hated the morgue. Even the lobby had a smell that resembled death or at least sanitized death. She spotted a woman sitting on the bench and assumed it was Vicki. Not many people hang around the morgue at 8am for fun. Walking up and extending her hand, Sarah introduced herself, "Vicki Donovan, I assume?" I am Lieutenant Sarah Carmichael and this is my partner, Amy Jones."

Vicki stood up to shake both their hands and Sarah noticed that she was a small woman, barely five feet tall and maybe one hundred pounds soaking wet. She had long blonde hair, pulled back in a ponytail, and small round eyes that conflicted with the shape of her face. She definitely didn't share many genes with Adam. "It's nice to meet the two of you," she said quietly, as low as a whisper, but enough for the Jersey accent to come through.

"I'm sorry for your loss," Amy offered with a friendly smile and sympathetic eyes.

"Thank you, but I haven't seen Adam in years. I don't think any of the family has. It has to be about 15 years now since I last saw him. He was never much into family. When he came to New York to start his business, he just never came back to Jersey. We heard about the trouble he got into with a past girlfriend, but that was it. None of us even had an address for him. I wasn't even able to send him birthday or Christmas cards. I guess he was happier being alone. Some people are like that, right?"

"I suppose so," Sarah replied. "It has been so long, are you sure you will be able to recognize him?" she asked, while guiding her towards the viewing room.

"You saw him Lieutenant. He was always a beautiful man. I am sure in death, his stunning features are still recognizable."

"If you are ready, I will have the curtain drawn back. If you need a minute that is fine."

"I am not here to grieve. Our family lost Adam, a very long time ago. I just want to be able to assist you in your investigation. Maybe, I consider it a parting gift to Adam since he never let any of us say goodbye."

Sarah pressed the button on the sterile, white wall, indicating that she was ready for the curtain to be drawn and the identification to be made. Adam was covered with a white sheet, with only his face viewable. They glanced over, and Sarah knew by the look on Vicki's face, that he was Adam Wright. The woman now knew her cousin was dead and could let the rest of the family have closure. "That's Adam. It's his unforgettable eyes. I am certain." Turning to Sarah, she said, "I have given my information to the front desk and they have arranged to have his body sent to New Jersey when it is released. May I go now?"

"I will sign the release as soon as possible so you can bury him. Thank you again for coming," she said, opening the exit door and watching Vicki Donovan walk through the parking lot. "Well, that was beyond useless. If I thought we had jack shit before, I was wrong. I am pretty sure we have even less right now. All we know is that we can't find one person he cared about or who cared about him. That really doesn't help the suspect pool." Frustrated, Sarah stomped out towards the cruiser.

"That may not be true," Amy responded, trying to catch up to her Lieutenant. "We still have to meet with his secretary. Sometimes a man's secretary knows things about him that even he didn't know."

Thinking about that, Sarah got behind the wheel and headed towards the office of Wright Construction. She had opted to do the interview that was somewhere comfortable for Adam's secretary, since she had seemed a little shaken up on the phone. She had rambled on and on about not knowing what to do with the business, how was she going to get paid, and oh yeah, poor Adam. She threw the last one in at the end of her blabbering rant of idiocy. From the sound of it, his secretary, Brandy Walters, probably knew more about shopping and hairstyles than she did about construction. Thinking about Wes' secretary, Jane Monroe, this meeting could prove informative. Jane practically ran Wes' schedule and life, for that matter. If Brandy knew even half as much about Adam, this meeting might actually give the investigation a lead.

Chapter 5

It rarely happened, but Sarah wanted to think, so she let Amy drive. Amy was the type of driver that thought the badge gave her special privileges, that 40 miles per hour meant 70 miles per hour. Today was no exception. She was weaving in and out of traffic, and thoroughly pleased she was the one driving. The sidewalks were crowded and most of the stores were advertising huge New Year's deals. It was hard to believe that it was the last day of 2019. Another year had come and gone, this one quicker than the last. More death occurred too. 2019 had brought a lot of blood and many bodies into Sarah's life. She closed her eyes and tried to get the image of death out of her head. She hadn't realized she had dozed off until she felt the car's parking break engage five minutes later.

They were parked in front of a grey and blue building. The big sign over the door displayed Wright Construction in big, black bold letters. They must be in the right place and in one piece, despite Amy's attempts at racecar driving. As she collected her notes to ready herself for the interview, she was interrupted by Amy's gasps for air and attempts at stifling laughs. When Sarah looked up and saw a tall, thin blonde woman coming out of the construction office, she knew what the laughing was about.

"Holy shit, it's plastic surgery Barbie," Amy let out while desperately trying not to make eye contact with the woman walking towards the car. "I got a hundred bucks that says if we dissected her, we wouldn't find one original part on that piece of work."

"That may be the case, but it's time to be professional. I swear to God, Amy, if you laugh in this woman's face, I am going to kick your ass. Get it out now and try to be a good detective. Shit, this is going to be harder than I thought. I can't keep my composure if you can't keep yours, damn it," Sarah said, stifling her own giggle. They got out of the car just in time to be face to face with Brandy Walters.

Brandy was standing at 5'9", due to the five-inch stiletto heels she was wearing. The heels, and her crotch-length shorts accented her long legs. She was wearing a very tight, white sweatshirt that grabbed her double-D breasts, which were without a doubt, not part of the original package. This woman was either blind or didn't know it was winter in New York. She missed that memo, along with quite a few others, judging by the looks of her. Her hair was platinum blonde, and her lips were almost the size of her breasts. She had a ton of make-up on, which was beginning to streak down her face from the tears.

"Thank you for taking the time to speak with us Ms. Walters. I am Lieutenant Carmichael, and this is Detective Jones."

"I just don't know what to do," she sobbed out. Her voice was almost as high as her shoes.

She turned around to walk them into the office, and Sarah noticed that she didn't walk, but instead, she pranced. Sarah could only think of how annoying this interview was going to be. They sat down at a desk in a conference room and Sarah went over what she could, regarding the case. She explained to Brandy where Adam was found, and that it was an open murder

36

investigation. "Do you know of any spots Adam frequented? Did he have a girlfriend? Do you know if he ever used the services of prostitutes?"

That question got Brandy's attention, although it was hard to tell what emotion she was feeling, since the overuse of Botox had left Brandy Walter's face looking permanently pouty. "Adam would never use a prostitute. Did you see what the man looked like? He was a god. He could have any woman he wanted," Brandy stated.

And there it was, the answer to the earlier question. This chick obviously knew nothing about construction. There was only one reason she was there, so Sarah came right out with it, "And let me guess, he wanted you and only you? How long were you and Mr. Wright having an intimate relationship?"

"We were in love, and have been since the moment we met," she squeaked out.

A little frustrated at the rate of conversation, Amy stepped in, "Which was when, Brandy?"

"Ummm," was all that came out as her eyes went towards the ceiling and a perplexed look covered her face. Sarah was worried that if this poor girl thought any harder, smoke might actually start to come out of her ears. A simple question had this girl looking like she was working out a complex calculus problem in her head. "I think like about, um, six months ago. Yeah, it was six months ago for sures."

"Well as long as you are 'for sures' about that, let's move on," Sarah quipped out and had to give Amy a warning glance about the grin on her face. "Can you tell us anything about him, his work, or your relationship?"

"I just answered the phones for him and I didn't do that very often. Whenever I was in the office, we always just fooled around in fun spots all around the office and then he, like, would tell me to call it a day. He always told me I was his best secretary." She said with a smile obviously reminiscing in her head.

Sarah prayed to God that the table they were sitting at wasn't in any of the images Brandy was remembering. Instinctively, she removed her hands from the table and scooted discreetly back. Just sitting in the chair was creeping her out now. She desperately wanted this interview to be over with. She felt herself losing brain cells the more she listened to Brandy speak. Steering towards ending the conversation, Sarah got right to the point, "Brandy, let me get this straight. You can't tell me anything about what Adam did or who he saw when you were not together? You can't tell me anything about his work and anyone who might have had a problem with him? You say you were in love, but the only love you had, occurred in various spots in this office and you really know nothing about him?"

"When you put it that way, it sounds cheap, and it so wasn't cheap," she said in her deafening, high-pitched tone. "We were in love."

"Thank you for your time. If you possibly think of anything else, please give me a call," Sarah said, handing Brandy her card. Sarah knew it was a long shot, as there clearly wasn't a lot of thinking going on with Brandy. Sarah rubbed her temples as she got up from her seat, and made her way outside. She looked at Amy and knew she was chomping at the bit to say something. "What?" Sarah blurted.

"You hurt her feelings, Lieutenant." Mimicking Brandy, Amy let her voice go as high as she could, "They were in love, and, like, their love, was, like, so not cheap. Geez, how did you not see that?"

"You are such a smart ass. You enjoyed that far too much. And yet again, we have nothing useful. Let's stop the presses. We have a guy who liked sex with big-breasted blondes that probably can't even tie their own shoes, which is why they wear those ridiculous heels. He was a loner. No family ties. No 'real' relationships, no friends, and no one who knew anything about him. None of this helps us catch his killer."

"Maybe we should go back to the prostitute angle. He didn't like relationships with people, but he obviously enjoyed sex. That's exactly what he could get from a prostitute. He could pay to get what he wanted with no strings attached. I mean, yeah, in the end he maybe got more than he bargained for, but maybe he was bored with Botox for brains back there and went looking for more fun for the night."

"I talked to the girls working the streets closest to the crime scene. No one remembered seeing him, Amy."

"We work daytime shifts. Most of those types of girls work night shifts. When you talked to them, it was a few of the daytime girls that were out working. If Adam picked up a girl the night he was killed, she probably works night shifts all the time, and those girls wouldn't know her. I think we need to interview the girls that work the evening shifts in the areas surrounding the hotel. I'm sure most of the girls work night shifts because it's better money right?"

Thinking about that, Sarah replied, "You may be on to something, let's get an officer out there to interview the girls around 11pm tonight. It can't be us tonight, because you and I are busy. You've got glam up Sarah duty this evening. I need you at my house at 6pm. The party starts at eight o'clock and you know it takes a lot of time to get me up to Virginia Porter standards."

"You make her sound so awful. I have met her twice now and she was very polite to me; not pretentious at all," was Amy's response as she got in the passenger side of the car. She could tell Sarah was only going to let her drive once today. From the look of irritation on her face, it seemed as if driving might be a good idea for Sarah to get her mind onto something else.

"That's because you aren't the one dating her son. To her, you are an officer of the law protecting our great city. I, on the other hand, am just the woman who doesn't fit her standards of what she expects for her son. She doesn't see me as an officer of the law. She respects you; she disdains me," Sarah whined as she drove through the congested New York streets, back toward the station.

"I'm pretty sure you're exaggerating it. It's been what, five years now for you and Wes? I am sure she accepts you by now."

Rolling her eyes, Sarah said, "Oh goody, five years in and I have yet to gain the acceptance of the mother of the man I love. That makes me feel so good. At least his Father is kind to me. He is such a sweet man. I honestly think Richard Porter likes everyone." Pulling into her spot at the station, Sarah got out of the car with Amy and headed in. She looked around and wondered why so many of the other officers used their personal vehicles. She always used her cruiser. The thought of parking her personal vehicle in the lot terrified her. For some reason, this particular lot had succumbed to someone with a graffiti addiction. Yet, considering it is a police lot with security cameras all around it, this determined artist did not seem deterred. Apparently, the other officers didn't think they could possibly be that one in one hundred the day they drove their personal vehicles in.

Entering the elevator, Sarah pushed the button to get to the bullpen and her office. "I am going to finish up some paperwork and call it a day. Schedule an officer to get out and talk to those girls tonight. Light a fire under their asses, and tell them to get me something useful. Head out after that and be at my house by six."

"Looking forward to it. Thanks again for getting me on the guest list. One of these days your invite is going to pay off and I am going to find me a rich husband," Amy said as she strolled off, smiling widely.

Sarah went into her office and finished her paperwork. She decided to call Wes before she headed out. When he answered his video chat, she could see he was having a rough day. "Looks like a killer of a day babe. If you are too swamped, we can forgo the party tonight."

"You always know how to make me laugh. Get that smile off of your face dear. We are going to the party tonight. You do not get off the hook that easily. I am just about wrapped up here, but yes, it has been a killer of a day."

"Don't you ever get worn out? Work all day and then party at night."

"I know you think you are sneaky, but you're not. In answer to your rather obvious question, no we will not be at the party all night. I just want to make an appearance with my beautiful girlfriend and show her off. Maybe an hour or two; I think you can handle it. It's right up your alley babe. Free endless drinks and those cute little finger foods you love."

Because he made her smile without even thinking about it, she grinned, saying, "You're a kiss-ass, giving me compliments and teasing me with endless drinks and food. You do know how to turn a woman on. Give me

41

enough drinks and I will be turning you on tonight," she said with a wink while turning to make sure no one outside her office heard her.

"I am holding you to that. I have to get back to work so I can get out of here in time, but I am having a car sent to pick you and Amy up at 7:30pm to bring you to my place. We can have a cocktail here before the limo arrives at 8:00pm. I figure showing up at 8:15pm is just early enough to not piss off my father, but just late enough to get my mother worked up."

"Oh how you know my weak spot. Keep talking dirty, it makes me so hot to hear you talk about infuriating your mother."

"I knew you would appreciate that. I will see you later, love you beautiful."

"Love y-," before she could finish her sentence, the video transmission had ended. She knew how busy he was, but she had wanted to keep him on the phone a little longer.

When she realized her phone call to Wes coinciding with her looking for more work was her way of procrastinating, she sighed loudly. She always did this to herself. She worked herself up about getting all done up and having to act and speak appropriately for an entire evening. Most of the time, it was for no reason at all. Besides the commonly snide comments from Virginia, everything usually went well, and it was all over with before she knew it. Hoping tonight would be the same, minus the snide comments; she got up from her desk and headed home.

Chapter 6

Sarah was just getting out of the shower when Amy rang the doorbell. She opened the door and let her in. "I can always expect you to be on time for these occasions."

Amy walked in with her dress in a bag over her shoulder, and a suitcase on wheels. Knowing the suitcase was full of hair and make-up items had Sarah's stomach clenching a little. She didn't mind make-up and getting dressed up at all. When she didn't have to live up to someone else's expectations, she thoroughly enjoyed playing with her hair and applying make-up. On nights like this, when it came to fancy and dealing with Virginia Porter, she always let Amy take care of it. They both walked into Sarah's bedroom and Sarah sat down at her maple wood vanity. It was a simple vanity and a bit dinged up from years and years of use, but it had been her mother's and she cherished it. She tried not to use it often, in order to preserve its life, but she loved to run her fingers along the edges of the worn wood. The crevices and grooves brought back pleasant memories of her as a child, watching her mother do her own make-up.

"I need to see your dress, so I can decide how I want to do your hair and make-up," Amy said as she walked over to where the new Barneys dress was hanging, still in the plastic bag Sarah left the store with it in. Amy pulled it out of the plastic and studied it. "Nice work. I am proud of you for picking out such a nice dress without my assistance."

"I am not a complete dysfunctional moron. I don't mind shopping or getting dressed up. I just like to do it

43

with zero expectations from anyone, that's all. It's the expectations of tonight that have me all unsettled and nervous as always. It's Wes, the promise of bottomless champagne and finger foods that has me ready to bite the bullet and face this evening's festivities." Feeling a little bit more excited than hopeless, now she was ready to start the glam up process.

Amy had all her toys sprawled out on the vanity. She grabbed the ceramic curling wand she had plugged in, and went to work on Sarah's hair. Thirty minutes later, her hair was done in beautiful golden curls. Amy then pinned the curls into a beautiful up do that left little wisps surrounding Sarah's strong and beautiful face. The hair was held into place with a lavish diamond hairpin in the shape of a flower. This final touch almost made it look like a tiara fit for a princess. The pin was made of real diamonds laid in a platinum setting and worth at least a couple thousand dollars. It had been a gift from Wes, one of the many, which she only wore when she went out with him. She loved the gifts because they were beautiful, but even more because it irritated Virginia that Wes spent that kind of money on her when it wasn't getting shown off enough. Wes, however, knew Sarah well enough to know that she didn't show anything off. He knew she loved them and that was all that mattered to him. Sarah also knew Wes well enough to know that he didn't need the gifts he gave to be shown off, he just wanted to make her smile. They came from very different backgrounds, but Sarah felt that they truly complimented each other well.

Sarah decided to put the base of her make-up on while Amy did her own hair. Tonight, Amy decided to let her long red hair down. She used a flat iron to straighten the slightly crimped ends from the braid she had in all day. It wasn't often she let it down and loose, but tonight her fiery red hair flowed down her back and the shine made it look alive.

Amy decided the make-up should stand out, but also be elegant at the same time. She had chosen to use mostly earth tones, but bring just a little accent to her eyes with a black pencil. She used this to bring out a depth in Sarah's deep-set eyes to show the intensity that sometimes was hidden behind the serious look she usually kept on her face. She had stunning blue eyes, but usually they were clouded with visions of death that she looked at everyday. But, not tonight. There would be no death or murder for her tonight.

"It's time," Amy said bounding around the room. "I can't wait to see your dress on you."

Sarah pulled her black evening gown out of the bag. She gently stepped into it and pulled it up over her perky bra-less breasts. The off-the-shoulder design made it a no bra dress and showed off her sexy toned arms. The dress swayed along the top of her feet as she turned to show it to Amy. She opened the small slit in the side of the dress and slid her thigh holster on. She secured her backup weapon under her dress and settled in. The mayor was kind enough to allow her one weapon on his grounds. Once she had her heels on, the dress would be the perfect length. She stepped into her satin, black and beaded heels. She couldn't afford the dress and new shoes, but then again, she hardly wore heels, so these felt new to her. They were very simple and strappy, with gorgeous diamond rhinestones around the ankle strap. She finished off the outfit with a simple pair of diamond earrings, another gift from Wes.

Amy smiled at her. "You look beautiful. Wes is going to love it. You did say a car was picking us up here and going to his place first right?"

"Yes, he knows how much you love his place. As a thank you for helping me get ready, he invited you for pre-party cocktails. Personally, I just think he wants me tipsy so he can take advantage of me tonight."

"That man can take advantage of me whenever he would like. No booze necessary. I would give my right arm to–"

Holding up her hand to shut Amy up, "For the love of God, don't finish that sentence." In response Amy's mouth opening to speak, Sarah just continued on, "the car will be here in ten minutes, you better get your dress on."

Amy's dress was as stunning as her hair. She chose a light blue halter dress with a severely plunging back line. It was sexy, but still elegant. It was skin-tight, to show off her toned body, but then opened up into a train around the back. She wore matching heels and carried a matching clutch. She chose an aquamarine earring and necklace set to complete it.

"Well Detective, don't you clean up nicely."

"I was serious when I said I was looking for a husband tonight," she laughed out. "You know me, I love getting dressed up and my sister always has all these designs that never got used.

Amy's younger sister had been a fashion student and was always designing dresses and outfits for classes that she never used. It seemed to benefit Amy since she was usually the model, and the clothes were exactly her size.

As Sarah was putting her badge in her small purse, the doorbell rang and Amy ran to answer it.

A pleasant young man in a nice suit stood at the door. "Your car is here madam. I will take you to Mr. Porter's house now."

"Thank you. You coming Lieute–," remembering their shift was over, Amy corrected herself, "I mean Sarah. Hard to get out of character sometimes, right?"

Getting out of character was cathartic sometimes, Sarah thought to herself. "I am ready. Let's go see how handsome my man looks tonight."

"Yummy," was all Amy said as they got in the car.

It was a nice drive to Wes' place. It was early on New Year's Eve and the streets were not yet jam packed, plus Wes and his parents lived in an area reserved for the more well to do folks. All the houses, if you could call ten room mansions houses, were gated and lined with ten-foot high walls. Wes' parents owned the biggest one on the hill, but Wes worked for most of his money, and chose one of the smaller homes in the neighborhood, with only six bedrooms. Why they call it a neighborhood still had Sarah baffled. The lots the houses sat on were so huge that you couldn't see any neighbors. The driveways were gated and no one parked on the streets. You would have to wait on the sidewalk outside someone's front gate and wait for them to pull out of their driveway in order to get a glimpse of a neighbor.

The driver pulled up to the large black, iron gate and pressed the security button. The car was cleared and against all of Sarah's instincts, she remained seated in the back until the driver came around to open the door for her. "Thank you," was all she said as they exited the vehicle. She looked up to find Wes waiting at the door to greet them, and as always, even after five years, her breath was taken away. His masculine beauty and penetrating eyes always managed to hit her right in the gut and make her a little light headed like a giddy schoolgirl.

She knew he was wearing an Armani suit, as that was his favorite. He went with all black tonight, and stood at the door with his hands in his pockets and a grin that would most certainly make any girl drool. It seemed to be working on Amy as well. She looked as if she may do just that. She couldn't take her eyes off of Wesley as he reached his hand out and grabbed Sarah's. He gently brushed his lips along her knuckles. "Good evening my stunning Lieutenant."

He then grabbed Amy's hand and gave it a gentle kiss. "Don't you look beautiful tonight as well Detective?"

Not sure if she could manage to formulate any other words without stuttering, so all Amy managed to say was, "Thank you."

Wes kept his home as simple as a home such as his could be. The furniture was modern, and he kept the artwork light. The majority of the interior design was done by a professional decorator, but his non-pretentious touch had gone into the decision-making. His home told people he was well off, but didn't need to flaunt it with tons of gaudy artwork and furniture that only had worth because of the price tag. "Ladies," was all Wes said as he led them into the parlor.

His parlor was nothing but his own. The room was simple, but screamed Wesley J. Porter. There was a large mahogany desk in the corner where his favorite picture of Sarah sat perfectly in the corner. He had an endless number of books on matching mahogany bookcases, with his fantastic wet bar placed in the middle. He kept his favorite types of brandy and scotch in the parlor for his favorite guests.

On the wall opposite his wet bar was his dartboard and shuffleboard table. He also kept his prized pool table in the parlor. The pool table had belonged to his great grandfather and had history with some of the most powerful men in New York in the last 100 years. Wes took great pride in the pool table being passed down to him. He spent a great deal of money keeping the wood, felt, and pockets preserved perfectly. He kept the original cues and balls in a glass display case and kept dozens of what he called "guest toys." He never let anyone, including himself, use the original cues or balls. In the middle of the room, there was a brown leather couch and two marble slab side tables. This is where Wes liked to sit and relax with a glass of Brandy after a long week. He gestured Sarah and Amy to have a seat and turned on music. It was a peaceful tune that Sarah had heard a hundred times sitting in this room, but still had no idea what it was called or who wrote it.

"I know Sarah will have brandy, but forgive me Amy for not remembering. Are you a brandy or scotch girl?"

"Actually, do you have a good whiskey?"

"A woman with fine taste. You will fit in nicely tonight," Wes replied as he poured her a tumbler of whiskey. He grabbed the small black gift box he had been hiding and handed the glass to Amy and the box to Sarah.

Sarah looked at him with shock in her eyes, "Not another freaking gift. I told you no more Wes. I can't keep up with all the gifts you give me and I can't wear most of them." She simply stared at him for a moment, holding the box in her hands. When he said nothing and only stared back at her, she knew arguing about the gift was pointless. He would never stop. She removed the white ribbon from the box and slid the black velvet top back. She wasn't sure who saw it first because she heard Amy gasp. Inside the box was a huge diamond on a long,

49

shiny chain. She knew Wes well enough to know that the only metal the chain could be was platinum, since that was his favorite.

The diamond was easily twenty-five carats and in a shape Sarah had never seen before. She picked it up and studied it in her hands. "Wes, it's absolutely beautiful and insanely huge." When he said nothing, she continued to study it and realized what the diamond was in the shape of. "It's a badge! You had the diamond made into the shape of a badge for me?"

"My cop wears one badge for the city and now another for me," he said and brushed his lips against her cheek, making her blush in front of Amy. He held his hand out and let her put it in his. He gently caressed her shoulders and neck, making his way behind her to slide the necklace on. He smiled when she grabbed her new badge and ran her fingers along it.

As soon as it was around her neck, she could feel the weight of it. It was stunning, but having something worth that much money around her neck made her nervous. She loved how much Wes knew her. He knew making it a badge would make her not want to argue about accepting it, and he made the chain long enough to hide the diamond between her breasts. She could wear it under her clothes and it could stay hidden if she chose.

"I knew you would appreciate it more if you could hide it," Wes said as he smiled at her and kissed her forehead. "You are wearing it out tonight until my mother sees it."

"Oh honey, I can do that for you, but only because you asked me to. I would never intentionally want to upset your mother," Sarah said with a devilish grin.

Amy had stayed quiet enough and let them have their moment. She couldn't stand it any longer, "Holy shit!

Let me see that thing." She pulled Sarah back down on the couch to get a closer look and her eyes almost bugged out of their sockets. "That thing could sink the titanic. I mean if some other rock already hadn't, but you get my point. I don't think I have even been near a diamond this big."

"It's too much and he knows it. That's why he has that shit eating grin on his face." Sipping her Brandy, Sarah played with her new gift awhile longer and instinctively tucked the necklace between her breasts. "I will pull it out when we get closer to your mother, but I don't want it showing in pictures. No one needs to see a cop wearing something like this. Not only will I get shit from the guys at the station for being all dolled up, but I will become a new target for jewelry thieves."

The security gate buzzed, letting them know the limo had arrived. The three of them walked out of the parlor and towards the front door when Sarah stopped Wes, just short of the front door. "Go ahead and get in the limo Amy. It appears my Lieutenant needs a moment with me. Help yourself to whatever you would like from the bar area."

"Sweet," Amy said and she bounced out the front door to the limo.

Sarah playfully pushed Wes against the wall and kept her hand on his chest. "Listen pal, just because you bought me a diamond the size of Wyoming, doesn't mean you are getting any tonight. I can't be bought, you hear me?" Softening her voice and bringing her lips just close enough to brush his, she continued, "Boozed up, yes, bought, no. But really Wes, thank you. It is the most beautiful thing I have ever seen."

"As are you," he replied, spinning her around and switching their positions. He pinned her against the wall with his body and drove his lips hard against hers. It lit up a passion so hot inside of her that she could feel the heat coming off her skin. He reached his hand up the slit in her dress and made his way up her thigh to his favorite spot. He stopped short when he heard her breath hitch and could feel the heat coming from inside her. I am glad you are pleased with your new badge. It is for me only."

"It has always been only you."

He smiled at her and continued his fingers up her thigh, and moved inside her. "God, I love the feel of you."

"Almost any other time, I would take this upstairs just to avoid the party, but my partner is in the limo." Feeling the large bulge coming from his pants, she smiled and said, "It appears you need a minute. I will go join Amy in the limo and make an excuse for you. Now if you don't mind, I am going to need you to put my panties back in place. She smiled at him, fixed her dress and took one last long look at him before she started out the door. "We will be finishing this later Wesley Porter."

"Thinking about that doesn't help with the current situation sweetheart," he said more to himself as Sarah was already out the door. He walked back into the parlor and poured another sip of Brandy. The Brandy did the trick and relaxed him as it made its way down his throat. He took one last hard swallow and headed out to join the ladies in the car.

Chapter 7

The limo was beautiful and the ride to the Porter Manor had been fun and full of levity. When they arrived at the gates, the limo was assaulted with bright flashes as the press tried to see who was inside. The Porter's New Years parties were always a huge event in New York. Getting a picture of Wesley Porter and his cop girlfriend seem to always make for exclusives and tons of gossip that Sarah didn't understand. *They were just people weren't they? Who the hell really cared what she did everyday or what Wes did.* She knew she would never get it and she assumed that was one of the reasons Wes loved her. She just didn't care. She loved him for him, not what he was or whose son he was.

The ride came to an end and the door was opened for them. Wes stepped out first and then escorted Amy out. She loved this part of the events she attended with Sarah and Wes. She posed and smiled eagerly for the cameras. Before reaching for Wes' hand, Sarah made sure her new diamond was safe and sound, tucked away from the camera lenses. They were not the only ones fashionably late. She noticed there were three other limos pulling in behind them.

Walking past the cameras on the long, red plush carpet, they stepped into a very large and extravagant foyer. The Porter Manor was very different from Wesley's home in a number of ways, starting with the décor. The foyer ceiling was roughly 25 feet tall and the space itself could hold Sarah's entire home in it. The floors were an imported Italian cmpress crème marble that was cut and laid in the pattern of 20x20 diamonds. It was so clean and shiny that you could almost see your reflection in them. The ceiling produced a 5-tier, 10-foot wide, marvelous crystal chandelier with gold accents that sparkled light from every angle. The room was broken up by a grand, double staircase that was framed with a custom decorative wrought iron railing that had beautiful details. Every wall was full of old world art worth millions, some newly acquired, but most were passed down through the years by the Porter bloodline. The home was the perfect setting for the lavish parties that were thrown there.

Tonight, the entertaining was to be done in the east wing of the home, where the ballroom was located. Having received a tour of the house before, she knew that the ballroom was off the foyer, down a long corridor to the left. To the right, down an equally long corridor, were the study, an office, and the gentleman's room where Mr. Porter kept all of his prized achievements and possessions. Straight back was the kitchen and two living quarters for the staff. The main bedrooms, all eight of them, were upstairs with five of the seven bathrooms. To top it off, the grounds also held a separate four-bedroom guest house next to the lake-sized pool in the backyard.

Wes took both Amy and Sarah's arms in his and escorted them through the foyer. Sarah had her eyes on one of the gentlemen carrying the trays of champagne, when she spotted Virginia and Richard Porter.

"Better get my money's worth babe. Pull the necklace out before my mother makes her way over here. And smile."

She plastered a larger than life fake smile on her face and slyly removed the necklace from its safe place. She felt the weight of it and the weight of the eyes on her as they stopped at the entrance to the ballroom, watching the Porters approach. She knew the instant Virginia saw the necklace. Virginia's composure was only affected for a moment before she recovered and kept her always camera-ready face smiling at Sarah.

Leaning in to kiss his mother's cheek, Wes said, "You look exquisite Mother, as always." He then grabbed his father's hand and gave it a firm handshake while signaling over with his free hand "You both remember Sarah's partner, Amy Jones."

"Of course we do. It's a pleasure to see you again. So glad you could make it to our little soiree." Virginia held up her hand, directing a waiter to bring a tray of champagne over to them. Sarah glanced at Virginia's short, brown hair that was slicked straight back and cropped perfectly at her ears. It was just enough to show off the large diamonds that adorned them tonight. She wore a pink, floor-length gown that was covered in lace and just barely came off the shoulders. Her neck was covered in pink and white diamonds that brought out the bit of gold she had in her brown eyes. Handing a glass to Sarah, she looked down at the jewel around her neck. "Well, that's some necklace. Looks as if my son has spoiled you with gifts, yet again." She may have said it with a smile, but the comment was dripping with disdain.

"Yes, I can't seem to get him to stop, no matter how many times I ask."

"He has always been a bit stubborn, and does what he pleases," replied Richard, breaking the tension a bit. "It is a stunning piece; almost as stunning as you two ladies look this evening. What a sight the two of you are." He kissed both women's hands with a warm smile.

No wonder he was a politician was the only thing Sarah could think.

Richard Porter was a stern looking man, until his smile lit up his face. He had deep-set blue eyes and a square jaw. He was tall and well built for his age. He always told people it was the football he had played in college that kept him looking so young. He was a handsome man with salt and pepper hair, and thanks to his good genes, it had not yet begun to recede or run away.

"You are always too kind, Mr. Porter," Sarah said as she sipped her glass of champagne. The room was full of people with glasses in their hands and snobbery in their eyes. Sarah watched some of the wives gather in a group and gossip about other wives. They tried to hide their moving lips behind their champagne flutes and divert their eyes when looked upon, but Sarah knew exactly what they were doing. They were judging others, and blatantly snickering. She noticed the snickering stop as eyes all around the room met with the diamond around her neck. All of the attention she was getting made her feel uneasy and twitchy. She couldn't tell if she was actually squirming or just fighting not to crawl out of her skin.

Seeing all the eyes on them himself, Wes knew how she would be feeling and interlocked his fingers in hers. "I know you need to make your rounds and greet the guests, so we won't keep you any longer. I am going to show these ladies a good time, mom," he said as he leaned in and kissed his mother's cheek. "Father," and he shook his father's strong hand while giving him a sincere smile. "Have a lovely evening, we will catch up later after you have made your rounds."

Virginia and Richard walked away, smiling and greeting more guests as they made their way around the room. It took everything Sarah had in her to keep herself from rolling her eyes in response to the fake smile Virginia had plastered on her face.

A very handsome, young waiter walked by with a tray of food, most items of which Sarah was unable to identify. She only knew that it was food and most likely edible, so she snatched a piece off the tray.

Amy did the same as the tray passed by her. "I have no idea what this is and I am pretty sure I don't want to, but yum!"

Wes held in a little laugh and replied, "No, you just enjoy it and maybe tomorrow I will tell you what it is." Knowing Amy would not want to know she was eating a snail, he just let her enjoy the moment.

"There are a ton of hot and eligible men in this room. I am going to go find my future husband." Amy flashed them a big smile and turned away to go find a man she might be able to tame.

"She is a keeper, Lieutenant," Wes said as he smiled and grabbed the champagne glass from Sarah's hand. Before she could protest he said, "There is more where that came from, but now I want you to look at me the way you were looking at that glass." He outstretched his arm as an invitation, "May I have this dance my love?"

"Only because you are so damn cute." She put her hand in Wes' and let him lead her to the dance floor.

He put his hand low enough on her back to have a few eyes flickering in their direction. He then slowly leaned in and nibbled on her ear as much for his own satisfaction as well as that of the gawkers.

"Mr. Porter, I do believe you are being inappropriate, as it seems we have an audience."

"You and I always seem to have an audience. It's no fun if we don't give them something to look at." To prove his point, he moved his hand down and cupped Sarah's butt perfectly in the palm of his hand. Getting the exact reaction he wanted from her, the onlookers, and his Mother, Wes laughed out loud and continued to push her around the dance floor.

They danced for a bit longer and then Sarah did her dutiful girlfriend role and mingled with people that mattered to Wes' work. She hated this part of the night the most, but did her best. It was hard to have a fake, interested conversation with people, when they spent the entire time staring at the diamond resting atop the fabric of her dress.

Sensing her restlessness, Wes kissed her cheek and said, "I know you are dying for a chance to hide that away from all the curious eyes. Why don't you go out to the terrace and get some fresh air. I will use that time to go mingle with my parents."

"Thank you so much. I don't think I can stand another minute of people staring at my breasts and then realizing it's not my breasts they are admiring." She giggled as he patted her on the butt when she turned away and headed outside for some fresh air.

She made her way through the sea of people and was relieved when she noticed no one else was on the terrace. Even with the outside heaters, it was a bit too chilly to be enjoyable. Sarah endured it, and took the opportunity to tuck away her new jewel into a safe spot, out of sight. She then paused a minute and breathed in the cold fresh air. Beneath the terrace was a large lawn and beautiful garden. It was barely visible with the little moonlight that snuck through the clouds, but she knew it was there. Just as she knew the grass went on and on and on. She wasn't quite sure how many acres the Porters lived on, but she knew it was a ridiculously large amount.

She took in one last cold, calming breath and headed back in to be by Wes' side.

* * *

As the night came to a close, there were fireworks, whistles, and screams of excitement when 2020 rolled in. The evening turned out to not be so bad after all, and Sarah shared a very romantic kiss with Wes when the clock struck midnight.

Soon after midnight, Wes led Sarah to say their goodbyes, and they headed off to drop Amy off at her house. After dropping off Amy, they headed back to Wes' house. In the limo, the privacy shield was in place, and Wes and Sarah had the entire car to themselves. Sarah had the next day off, so she took advantage of it by having more champagne from the bar stock in the limo.

"I love getting you drunk, Lieutenant," Wes said as he slid across the seat, rubbing his hand up her leg.

"You never have to get me drunk. You can have your way with me whenever you want, Mr. Porter." She winked at him as he slid her dress up, exposing her long legs. He brought his hand to her leg, and made his way up her thighs. He was pleasantly surprised to feel that Sarah wasn't wearing any panties. Instantly, he became hard as he began to caress her warm, moist area. Sarah leaned in and kissed him passionately as he slid his fingers deep inside her. She let out a small gasp and moved her hand over the top of his pants stroking his member wildly. After a few moments, she pushed him back against the black, leather seat and straddled him. He pulled down her gown, exposing her soft, perky breasts and as he slowly tantalized her nipples with his tongue, she began to grind back and forth on top of him. Just when Wes was about to remove his pants and ravage her, the limo came to a stop. "Time to continue this in the house," Sarah whispered in his ear as Wes tried to discretely climb out without the driver noticing the bulge in his pants.

As they entered the house, Sarah wasted no time. She stood in the hallway and dropped her dress to the floor. Even in the dark, Wes could still make out the perfect curves of her body. As he approached, she leaned against the wall and beckoned him closer with a sly grin. He pulled the last of his clothes off and as he got within an inch of her body he could feel the heat pulsating off her skin. He leaned in and filled her mouth with his tongue in a long, passionate kiss that left her begging for more. He firmly grabbed her by the waist and turned her around, pressing her forcefully against the wall. She felt a flutter in her stomach as this was out of character for Wes. She could hear her own breath catch and hold in her lungs, as she waited in anticipation for what was to come next. Within seconds, he wrapped his hand around her chest, cupping her left breast tight as he pulled her in close. She could feel his sex pressing hard against the bottom of her butt, pushing through to find his way inside her. When he finally entered, she released the breath she had been holding in and pushed back hard against him so that he was now deeper inside her. He continued to thrust in and out of her, with a relentless strength, his hand now leaving her breast and making its way to her clit. She moaned out in approval as he rubbed his fingers back and forth on her.

As he leaned in and gave her a few bites on the neck, she could take it no more. She let out a long whimper as she felt herself climax. Wes thrust himself inside her a few more times and released as well. They stood in the hall dripping with sweat and panting from pleasure. Wes then scooped Sarah up and carried her off to bed.

Chapter 8

Lucy sat at her vanity in her tiny rented studio and stared at herself in the mirror. It had been a week since she had last worked. A week since she had killed that man in his car. She was relieved that she hadn't heard anything about it except that it was an accident, even though she knew it was murder.

A murder she had committed.

A murder she had enjoyed committing.

She stared through her own reflection as she remembered strangling the old man and watching him take his last breaths as he fought for life. She remembered all the blood as she repeatedly stabbed that once handsome man who she had taken a liking to.

No one could place her with Adam Wright or the older man. That's why she chose to stay a loner and not talk to the other girls. She didn't want to know anyone, and didn't want anyone to know her. Her need for anonymity had been a lifesaver.

So why had she waited one week before working again? She kept telling herself that everyday life just got in the way. She knew better. She knew it was being typical that scared her. Could she go out and please one John after another, knowing what she was capable of? She didn't know if she was more worried about controlling herself, or missing the adrenaline rush that she felt when she took a life. The world was better off with those men gone. A couple less perverts in the world, she kept telling herself.

If she wasn't so broke, another night off might have been in the cards for Lucy Lust. She just wasn't sure if it was a good idea to let herself back out on the loose, so soon.

Too late to worry about it now, she thought. She had her short, cropped black wig on. The hair fell just below the ears. It was shiny jet black with red highlights. It was a new year and she was going for a new look. Tonight's office wear was a black and red skin tight corset to match her hair. She accompanied it with a black silk skirt, black stockings and black thigh-high boots. It was cold, but she needed money and knew the short skirt would get her more of that than pants would. The boots would have to be enough to warm her. She selected three temporary tattoos tonight. Placed strategically above her left breast was a blue butterfly. On each wrist was the words "live for today." She didn't choose to have tattoos in her everyday life, but she loved to be able play with them and change them up when she worked nights.

Her goal tonight was to make enough money to get out of the hole and go home. Maybe some normalcy would be good for her. Maybe her old routine could bring her back mentally from where she had gone since the killings. An hour later, Lucy had taken care of two Johns and let them go on their way. She hadn't gotten that disgusted feeling that gave her an urge to hurt them. She was feeling pretty good, when another guy walked up to her.

He was a short, balding man with a rather innocent smile. His face was round and his cheeks were flushed. When he spoke, Lucy could tell he was nervous. That meant he was a newbie to paying for sex; at least sex with a human being. From the looks of it, he paid for a lot of sex that he only got to watch from the chair in front of his computer. He whispered when he asked her, "Do you do appointments with clients at Unbind Your Mind?"

Lucy had only been to that place a couple of times, but she remembered it well. It was a fetish club that allowed the client to pick their fetish, and a room was created just for that fetish. The walls were covered with projection screens that could change the image of the room at anytime. They offered an endless amount of sex, fetish, and bondage toys. They claimed to be able to make any fantasy come true. She wondered what his fantasy would be.

"I accompany clients there, but the price depends on what you want."

"I want you to dominate and beat me into submission for the weak little man that I am," he said in a whisper, but Lucy could still hear the excitement in his voice.

So much for a typical night she thought to herself.

"I can do that for you. Meet me there in fifteen minutes."

"Thank you mistress." The bald little man smiled and ran off.

It was cold, but she preferred not to be seen walking with a John and wasn't quite comfortable to get in the car with one yet. Her first two Johns of the night had just wanted quickies with her mouth in a privacy booth in one of the popular nightclubs nearby. The legalization of prostitution hadn't happened, but the clubs tried to make it safer for the girls who chose to work. They offered privacy rooms in the back of the clubs and only expected tips on the way out. Most of the nightclubs did this, but the ones that frowned upon it made it known.

Ten minutes later, she was in front of Unbind Your Mind. It was a large industrial building that took up its own corner. There was parking in the front and the rear of the building. Unless you were ready to unbind your mind or bind your body, you wouldn't know what the inside was about. There was a sign on the front door indicating that the store was for adults above the age of 18 only. There were no cameras and they didn't check ID, so they just assumed who was or wasn't 18, but it seemed to work. Lucy had never heard of any complaints regarding the store. Anonymity is what kept a place like this popular; and anonymity, she could respect.

She pushed her way through the doors and saw the bald little man waiting for her.

"I already told them what I wanted and the room is being set up now." He must have felt more at home here as he was now speaking loudly and almost jumped with joy as he walked. "Follow me," he said with an eerily chipper voice. They proceeded down a dark, black hallway that was lit with a soft hint of red from the specially colored bulbs that hung in the gothic sconces on the wall. After a couple moments, they entered into what seemed like the twilight zone to Lucy. It was a tiny room that couldn't have been more than 400 square feet in size. On the walls were the projections of a classroom. It wasn't your typical classroom, as the ceiling held a sex swing hanging down in the center of it. There were many chains and straps added for the multiple angles of bondage that it provided. Nailed on one of the walls was a case that shelved whips in many sizes, shapes and textures, along with many objects for insertion purposes. Lucy glanced over to the small, tight leather outfit that hung on the wall. It was black with white trim, and as she got closer, she realized it was a very different take on a nun's uniform. The theme of the evening was starting to sink in, so she glanced at the awkwardly giddy man and said, "What will it be?"

"Well," he said, rubbing his hands together. "I really need some discipline. Can you come up with some creative ways to punish me?" he said with wide, excited eyes.

"I think that can be arranged," she said. He opened his wallet and handed her $250, "Make it good and don't hold back, I've been a really bad boy." This would be the best $250 she would ever make. Lucy slid over to the corner and worked for at least ten minutes, trying to squirm her body into the tight leather nun suit that had been provided for her. Finally, fully immersed in the tight, shiny costume that allowed her no room to breathe, she was ready. The tiny bald man had already positioned himself in the swing. He was naked with his ass to the ceiling, waiting patiently for his beating. Thinking about how uncomfortable the outfit was, and how hard it was for her to breathe, she was ready to give it to him. For the next hour, Lucy spanked, pinched, and probed every inch of that man's body till he was covered in welts and beaming with happiness. If only all of her Johns could be this easy. He thanked her profusely and said he would love to see her again. She exited the club and made her way back onto the street.

That certainly was an interesting way to spend part of the evening, she thought. Definitely not typical, but it took Lucy's mind off other things. She walked down the street towards her studio when a man walked up beside her.

"You still on the clock tonight, honey?" he asked and grabbed her ass.

"I can squeeze in one more, since you were such a gentleman in asking," she replied sarcastically.

"Didn't know you girls were easily offended. Anyway, I just want a blow-job. My car is parked around the corner. That's a quick last bit of money for you tonight."

Lucy was happy he didn't want to play games. She had her fill of games for the night. He was straightforward, knew what he wanted, and asked for it.

He was an ordinary man with a very forgettable face. He had brown hair, brown eyes, and not even a hint of a smile. He was around 6'5" tall, and about 190 pounds. He wasn't a big man, but he wasn't necessarily a small man either. He also wasn't an ugly guy, but he wouldn't be considered attractive. She followed him around the corner to his car and they got inside.

He sat in the driver's seat and pulled his unzipped pants to the floor. He wasn't all the way hard yet, but enough to let Lucy know he was ready.

"It's all yours toots," he said as he grabbed the back of Lucy's head and brought it closer to his lap.

Lucy stroked him with her hand and her mouth. He moaned in pleasure and she felt him growing in her mouth.

"Tell me you like it baby. Tell me how big I am," he said.

All she could think was, do you want me to do this or do you want me to talk to you. How easily men forgot what they wanted. Yet, men think women are indecisive. But, she obliged and muffled out the words while performing the task she was being paid for.

"That's it baby. I'm close." As he was getting more excited, his grip tightened on the back of her head and he kept forcing her head down on him, causing her to choke. She tried several times to bring her head up and get air in, but he kept ramming himself into the back of her throat. "Oh yeah, daddy is gonna give it all, right down the back of your throat. Just another minute and it's all yours."

Fighting for air, Lucy smacked his leg, but he only tightened his grip, repeating how close he was. As she begun to get light-headed and see stars, her rage kicked in. There was no keeping it back, and it exploded out of her. She bit down on him so hard, he began screaming in agony. As his demeanor changed to that of a screaming child, she sat up and punched him square in the jaw. That made the screaming stop, but as she moved to put her hands around his throat, he got his composure.

"You stupid fucking cunt," he screamed. "My dick is bleeding." Wiping the blood from where his lip had split open, he leaned over and slapped her in the face. It was with an open hand, but it made her see stars. She fell back into the passenger side window and heard the thud of her head on the glass.

He came at her again, gripping at her pockets and feeling all over her body. She was pretty sure he was looking for identification because he could have hurt her at any point. He had a hold of part of her skirt as she struggled to get out of the car. She managed to get the door open and fell out onto her butt. He was still leaning out the car, trying to get a hold of her. She kicked out, and the heel of her boot hit him in the chest. She heard him gasp for air, and she took the opportunity to get to her feet and started running.

"I will find out who you are bitch," he shouted after her. "I will find you and you will pay for this."

She ran a mile out of the way of her studio to make sure she wasn't being followed. When she was sure she was alone, she turned the corner to her apartment and walked towards the entrance. She took one last look around and keyed in the entrance code. She climbed the steps to her apartment, unlocked the door and stepped in. She closed the door and just slid to the ground, using the door as leverage. She couldn't stand on her shaky legs any longer.

What had happened to her? She used to be able to do this every night and deal with whatever the Johns wanted. She would take any request and serve it up with a smile. After all, it was just sex, and she needed the money. But, it was so much more than that now. When she got dressed up as Lucy, she let herself become someone completely different. This new Lucy had a rage she didn't know was inside of her before. She was capable of things she once thought of as morally and definitely legally wrong. She knew prostitution was breaking the law, but murder and assault were different. Prostitution was frowned upon, but murder was a capital crime in New York.

She put her head in her hands and rubbed her eyes. *What is happening to me?*

Chapter 9

Sarah awoke in her bed alone. The New Year had brought on new deadlines for Wes, which kept them apart for almost a week already. She managed to meet him for lunch two days prior, on her day off, but had not seen him since. She was very independent and appreciated her alone time, but she was beginning to miss him. She rolled over in bed and grabbed her robe off the floor where she had left it when she had collapsed into bed.

Thinking of Wes, she walked over to her vanity and took out the diamond badge he had given her. She slipped it around her neck. She rubbed her fingers over it, vividly remembering the wonderful night they had spent together on New Year's Eve. Feeling her heart start to race and a slight quiver between her legs, she put the thoughts away and slid the necklace beneath the robe. She didn't need to see it to know it was there and to appreciate the love the man that had given it to her.

This morning it was a toss-up of what was more important: coffee or a hot shower. She decided to do both. She made a cup of coffee and took it into the shower with her. Water trickled down her back as she rested her head against the shower wall and let the steam clear her sinuses. The coffee was gone before the shower was over, and the thought of a second cup had her turning the shower off quickly. She would have one more cup of coffee and then she would get dressed and head out the door for today's shift.

It was a cool day in New York, but the sun was still shining in the clear blue sky above and there was oddly enough, less traffic than usual. That was something that rarely happened in her neck of the woods, but Sarah found herself pulling into her spot at work ten minutes early. Since Amy was always early, they ended up pulling in at the same time.

"Fancy meeting you here Lieutenant," Amy joked with a big smile.

"How, the hell, are you so chipper in the morning? It's annoying. I can't even be that chipper after eight cups of coffee."

They rode in silence as the elevator took them up to their floor, but Amy couldn't keep it in any longer. "So, I noticed you have been wearing your necklace under your clothes," Amy mentioned. Noticing Sarah look down, she whispered, "I can see the chain just under your collar."

"I like to wear it, but I just don't need anyone to see it and give me a hard time. I don't want anyone to know about it. Got it?"

"Yes, Ma'am." As they entered the bullpen, bodies, and loud noises surrounded them.

"Go grab me a donut and meet me at my office," Sarah ordered and walked away. She was a couple feet from her door when she saw a tall, lean man at her door. He was wearing blue jeans and a black colored shirt. She recognized him, but couldn't put a name to his face.

"What can I do for you?" She let the rest of the sentence hang so he could introduce himself.

"Detective Bell, Aaron Bell."

Sarah unlocked her door and walked into her office. "C'mon in. What can I do for you Detective Bell?"

71

"We started working a case that looked like an accidental death, but through interviews and investigation it appears it may be a homicide."

"And what brought you to that conclusion?" She accepted the file he handed her and noticed it was the autoerotic asphyxiation case she had heard all the guys talking about. She read the file and listened to the detective at the same time.

"Since our victim, Frederick Hoyt, died in such a way we thought it would be wise to canvas the streets nearby and talk to some of the working girls that possibly cater to that sort of request." He cleared his throat when Sarah looked up from the file, urging him to go on. "It appears he did like to pay for some of their services. He had a regular girl he liked to use, Trixie, I believe. But, she wasn't available that night. We have confirmed her alibi. According to some of the other girls, they saw his car that night and they are pretty sure he picked up some other girl. None of them can tell me anything about her, but she may be a witness or person of interest. My Lieutenant was informed of your current open case in which it is assumed a prostitute killed Mr. Wright. He asked me to bring you the case file and find out how you want to proceed."

She finished reading the file and looked up, "You sure don't have much. His regular girl was busy so he decided to park and take care of himself. He misjudges what he can handle and dies. Not much here that screams homicide."

"Yes Ma'am." He started to rise and grab the file off the desk, but Sarah placed her hand on it first.

"I will look into it further Detective Bell." By the look of relief on his face, she imagined his Lieutenant was a hard-ass.

"Thank you." He turned to walk out the door and ran right into Amy. "Oh my god, I am so sorry."

Amy was pissed and flustered, as she watched her files fall to the floor, "Jesus Christ, watch whe–" she started, until she looked up and saw who ran into her. "It happens, no worries, the donuts are fine," she giggled out and gave him a flirty smile. Amy stopped talking, as she realized she wasn't making much sense.

"My apologies again," he said as his cheeks flushed and he gave Amy a huge smile.

Amy made eye contact with Sarah and made a face that let her know she wanted to be introduced.

Sarah rolled her eyes and said, "Detective Bell, this is my partner Detective Jones."

Amy offered her hand out, "It's a pleasure to meet you Detective. You can call me Amy."

"And vice versa, you can call me Aaron," he replied as he accepted Amy's soft, small hand into his with a firm handshake.

As they continued the overly long handshake, Sarah broke in, "Aaron is here giving us a new case to follow. There's a possibility of foul play involved in the autoerotic asphyxiation case we heard about."

"Super. I mean, it's not super he is dead. I just mean super, we get to work on it."

Noticing Amy starting to babble, Sarah jumped in, "Thank you Detective Bell. We will keep you abreast of any new leads if it turns out not to be a homicide case."

"Thank you Lieutenant, I appreciate it. It was really nice meeting you Amy." With another big smile, he turned and walked out of the office.

"Oh my god, was I a total idiot?" Amy set the donut on Sarah's desk and sank down into the chair. "When I looked up and saw how cute he was, I freaked a little. This is why I don't have a boyfriend. I can't even have a normal conversation without getting all nervous and stuttering. As always, you had to jump in and save me."

"Calm down. You weren't a total idiot. Maybe just a partial idiot." Amy shot her a look of desperation. "I am just kidding. You were fine. Now, shall we get to work? We can discuss your personal life later."

"Easy for you to say, your personal life is like a fairy tale." Amy sulked a little and snickered out, "I hate you. There, I got it out. We can work now."

"Well gee, thank you Detective. I am so glad we work on your time schedule. That was your only emotional meltdown of the day allowed. She handed the new case file over to Amy, "What do you think?"

"It's not too far of a stretch. If this turns out to be murder, we have two cases involving prostitutes as the possible suspects."

She let Amy finish reading the file when her desk phone rang. She picked it up and heard shouting on the other end. She listened to the desk clerk explain what was going on and told him she would be down in a minute.

"I could hear all that from over here," Amy said. "What's going on downstairs?"

"Apparently a guy downstairs came in to report an assault, but refuses to leave until someone from homicide talks to him." She grabbed her pepper spray and handed it to Amy. "He claims it was not assault, but attempted murder and will not leave until he can report it that way. Let's see if he sings the same tune once he sees he gets stuck with me. Let's go."

Sarah shut the door to her office and headed down in the elevator with Amy. She could hear the shouting and officers asking him to calm down before the elevator opened.

"The bitch would have killed me if I hadn't fought back," the man shouted. He was tall and had a hard face. His brown eyes were dark and angry. He had his brown hair covered with a baseball cap and was wearing blue jeans with an ordinary white shirt. His face was distorted with anger and his mouth wouldn't close long enough for anyone to say anything to him. "It wasn't assault. She would have killed me. She wanted to kill me. I could see it in her crazy eyes."

Sarah stepped off the elevator and met eyes with the man. "I am Lieutenant Carmichael, Homicide Division. What can I do for you Sir?"

"Those fucking eyes. You have the same fucking eyes as that cunt." He stormed toward her and was immediately restrained by several officers. He continued to shout, "Show me your wrists. I can prove it. You are the whore from last night. You tried to kill me."

Amy stepped up and looked the man in the eyes, "She is a Lieutenant in the New York Police Department, not a prostitute, and she deserves more respect from you than that. Call her that one more time and you will be locked up for disorderly conduct."

"It's okay Amy. Let's make him feel better and validate that his accusations are false." Sarah walked up to the man and unbuttoned the cuffs of her collared shirt. She rolled each sleeve up and showed him her wrists. "I have no tattoos and have a full time job with the police force. I assure you I am not a prostitute and did not try to kill you Mr.—"

"Keith. My name is Keith Simon." He was starting to calm down now and just looked confused. "She had the same eyes as you and the same build. Her eyes were green but they had the same intensity as your blue ones. She had black hair, but right away you reminded me of her. She had a butterfly tattoo above her breast. Let me see your chest."

The room fell silent. Wanting to prove a point, she was tempted to unbutton her shirt and show him there was no butterfly anywhere on her chest, but she remembered the huge diamond she had beneath her shirt. "I will forget that you have admitted to using the services of a prostitute, which is still illegal, if you take my word for it about no tattoo and forget about me showing you my chest. I can promise you that won't happen in your lifetime."

"You care about filing charges for soliciting, but not about attempted murder," he spat out.

"You haven't given me a chance to care. Instead, you called me a whore and tried to get me to take my shirt off."

Realizing how that sounded and also realizing that officers surrounded him, he relaxed. "Fine, you're right. I apologize, but I don't take it lightly that a whore attacked me. I want her found and to pay for what she did."

"You can explain to my partner exactly what happened. She will listen and start a report for you. From there, we will do what we can to find out who this woman is. Officers, one of you take him to interview room number one please. Detective Jones will be with you in a moment, Mr. Simon." Gesturing Amy to come to her, she walked to the side of the main lobby.

"You okay, Lieutenant? You look a little pale."

She leaned against the wall and rubbed her temples. "I am fine. It's not everyday you get accused of being a hooker and attempted murder. Go take his statement and we will look into it, if it seems there is anything to look into. This guy gave me a headache. I am going to take five and get to work. Meet me in my office when you're done with his statement."

"I don't mean to point out the obvious, but that makes three."

"What makes three, Detective?"

Sensing Sarah's mood, she thought about just dropping it, but the look she got said spit it out already, so she did. "If this guy isn't completely off his rocker and the other case is connected, that makes three. Two homicides and an attempted murder all by a prostitute, and possibly the same one."

"That's a lot of ifs Detective. Get the statement and we will move forward from there." She turned before Amy could say anything else and headed to the elevator. She stopped at the vending machine and grabbed a bag of chips and a soda. She had been looking forward to the donut, but it was probably stale from sitting on her desk so long. The chips would have to do. She took the snacks to her office, closed the door, and closed her eyes. Her head was beginning to pound, and she knew if she didn't get it under control, it would turn into a full-blown migraine.

What a way to start the day, she thought.

Chapter 10

Keith Simon sat, fuming in the interview room they left him waiting in. He stared at the one-way glass, knowing that they were there behind it, staring back at him and laughing at how weak he was to let a woman do this to him. He knew those damn cops wouldn't believe him. Just because a whore had attacked him didn't mean he couldn't take any of these low rent cops that thought they could put their hands on him. If it weren't for the utter shock of what that whore did, he would've ripped her throat out. He wasn't going to hold back now. If they weren't going to take him seriously, then he would take justice into his own hands. That little bitch was going to pay.

He was going to file his complaint, let the cops find her, and then he was going to take matters into his own hands. He smiled, thinking about holding her down and ramming himself into her just to show the bitch that a little bite wouldn't keep him from getting what he paid her for. He could see it now, so clearly in his head. He would gag the whore to keep her quiet. Then, he would pin her hands with one of his while the other jammed him inside of her. Once he was in, he would not be gentle. He would use his now free hand to wrap around her throat. In his head, he watched her eyes well up with tears as he thrust harder and deeper inside of her. With each thrust, he would tighten his grip around her neck until she stopped squirming and took her last breath. He knew he would climax when he watched her shed her last tear and take the last breath she would ever take. He would reach his climax while she reached her end.

He was still visualizing his fantasy and had to fight off an erection as the petite detective walked in. The smile vanished from his face and he looked hard and angry again. "It's about time," he complained. "I have a life to get back to."

Most likely, a life of torturing animals and scaring young children was all Amy thought when looking at him. She plastered a fake smile onto her face and introduced herself. "I am Detective Jones. Sorry for making you wait. I just wanted to make sure I had everything so we can get you out of here as soon as possible."

"Good, let's do this. I want this bitch found."

"I am sure you do Mr. Simon. Let's begin," Amy said, grabbing a notebook and pen. "Just walk me through everything you remember."

He went through the incident, including where he had been prior, and where he went afterwards. He included the time and place from beginning to end. He gave a description of the woman who attacked him, and as he did, he became more agitated.

Picking up on his anger, Amy tried to calm him a bit. "Mr. Simon, please be advised that we will do everything in our power to investigate this and bring your attacker to justice. Any justice you try to take into your own hands can be punishable by the full extent of the law." Holding her hand up to keep him from interrupting, she continued, "The NYPD takes every crime very seriously. We do what we can to protect all the civilians in our fine city. We will take your complaint just as serious and do all that we can for you. Do you understand Mr. Simon?

"Yeah, yeah, I got it. You don't want me to find the whore and deal with her myself. Do your job and I won't have to," he said as he stood up. "So, are we done here?"

"Yes sir, we are. Thank you for your time." Amy held out her hand, but he ignored her, grumbled to himself, and walked out the door.

Being very grateful that interview was over, Amy headed to Sarah's office to fill her in. She got there just in time to hear Sarah getting off the phone with dispatch. "Mr. Simon's complaint will have to wait. We've got a homicide at a car dealership uptown."

"Can you pull the car up front and I will meet you?" Amy asked. "I haven't had anything to eat yet today."

"Do what you want, but from what dispatch said, it's a nasty one. The first one on scene sounded pretty shaken up."

"Great, there goes my appetite." Amy stepped in stride with Sarah and headed for the elevator.

Amy filled Sarah in on the complaint from Keith Simon as they rode the elevator down and got into the car.

"I am putting Frederick Hoyt above him on my list."

"That should piss Mr. Simon off a little."

"I am pretty sure Mr. Hoyt is a little more pissed off, considering he is dead. If this Keith guy wants to go get himself murdered he can move up on my list."

Amy laughed and remembered why she loved working with Sarah so much. Not only had Sarah been her trainer and now partner, but also, they were friends. She loved that she could appreciate Sarah's dry humor. Some of the other cops couldn't. "So, any details on what we are heading to? Prep me a little," Amy said.

"All I heard was it was messy and identifying the victim is going to be difficult."

"Fantastic. I am really glad you gave me a heads-up and I didn't eat."

They pulled up to the car dealership. There was already a crowd behind the yellow tape and one local news crew was already in place. Before they could even get out of the car, Sarah knew the news reporter recognized her.

"Lieutenant," the tall blonde shouted with her cameraman behind her. "What can you tell us? It must be a homicide since you are here."

"No comment," Sarah sneered out. "Now, please get out of my way so I can do my job." Briskly walking by the reporter, she signed in with the officer securing the scene. "Who was first on scene?"

"Officers Kline and Roberts, ma'am," the obviously green officer replied. "They are in the car wash bay in the back, with the body."

Sarah glanced at his uniform to get his name. "Thank you, Officer Lovato. Keep all these people back and I don't want to see a camera anywhere near here."

"Yes ma'am," was all he said, but Sarah hardly heard him as she had already crossed under the tape.

They were headed around the lot, and before they even rounded the corner, they were assaulted by the horrific smell of burning flesh. Amy winced and covered her mouth and nose. "Oh God, you just never get used to that."

"Suck it up Detective. Let's get this over with." Sarah looked around, took it all in, and turned to locate the first on-scene officers. She held out her hand to introduce herself to both officers.

Roberts was a small man, maybe in his twenties. He looked like he had come right off the farm and at this moment, was probably wishing he were back home. He looked pale and his eyes were puffy.

Officer Kline was a tall, forty-something year old woman with a stern look. She had veteran written all over her. The scene had not caused her face to lose any of the color, or her eyes to show concern for Roberts.

"Fill me in," Sarah said, staring at the burned body. It was hanging from one of the machines in the car wash bay with a chain around the ankles. Not only would the fire make identifying the body difficult, but the fact that there was no head in sight would really make it a tough one to solve.

Officer Kline began giving the preliminary report. "The dealership doesn't open until 10am but the receptionist comes in at 8am to open, and the manager shows up around 9am. According to the Manager, Sheldon Blake, the doors were still locked when he arrived. He walked in, looking for the receptionist, Cynthia Hopson, and when he couldn't find her inside, he looked for her outside. When he walked out back, he could smell a horrible smell coming from the car wash bay and he walked back to find out what it was. That's when he saw the body hanging from the wax machine. He states that he did not touch anything and called us right away. He said that after he called us, he tried several times to call Mrs. Hopson, with no success. At this point, the body is unidentified, but he thinks it's hers. We did an initial sweep of the premises and have not been able to locate a head."

"Thank you Officer Kline. I would like to talk to Mr. Blake."

"He is in the break room inside, waiting for you Lieutenant."

"Amy, I want to look around a moment. Get Mr. Blake to get you the personnel file for Cynthia Hopson. Get her address and send a uniform to her place." Amy walked away and Sarah looked around the scene. She wondered if the head would be found close by or if it had been taken as a souvenir.

Photographs of the scene were being taken as the medical examiner arrived. He prepared to take the body down and had to move back when bits of flesh fell to his feet. Sarah could only think of how nice it was that she didn't have to do that part of the job. She walked past the medical examiner before heading inside to meet Sheldon Blake. "Will you get me time of death as soon as you have it," she asked the medical examiner.

Today, Molly Brightwood was the examiner on scene. She was a small woman with a brown ponytail and glasses. She never seemed to smile, but in her line of work, who would? "Sure thing Lieutenant, but it will have to wait until I get back to the lab. The heat from the fire is going to mess up the internal temperature. I am going to need to open her up."

"Her?" Sarah wasn't sure how anyone could tell the sex of what remained hanging from the chain.

"If you look closely at the pelvis, you can see the sacrum is tilted back, the ilium is spread wider, and the pelvic outlet is bigger than that of a male. These are all indicators that this is a female. I will need to remove the remaining flesh and clean the bones to try to get you race and approximate age. Finding her head would help," Molly said gently, lifting the burnt hand. "Fingerprints are going to be a bitch."

83

"Working on it Doc." Sarah left the doctor to do her job and headed inside the car dealership. She found an officer in with Sheldon Blake and excused him. "Thank you, Officer." For a handsome and well-built businessman in a suit, Sheldon was crying like a baby. "Mr. Blake, I am Lieutenant Sarah Carmichael. I need to ask you a few questions."

He wiped his eyes and tried desperately to catch his breath. He attempted to stop sobbing, but only continued again. "I know it's her, I know it's Cynthia," he wailed out in between sniffles. "Oh god, she is really gone. What am I going to do?"

"We do not have a positive ID yet. I have officers trying to locate Mrs. Hopson. Was she married, does she have friends we can call, anyone who might know if she is missing?"

Instantly, Sheldon shot out of his seat. His eyes were wide now, and he had complete control as he shouted, "You keep that bastard away from this place. He did this to her, he killed her and displayed her like this for me to find. That man is a monster."

"Calm down please, Mr. Blake." Sarah looked at Amy and recognized the nod that let her know the officers were unable to locate Cynthia Hopson. The parts that were left of her were most likely being taken to a lab right now. "Mr. Blake, how long have you and Mrs. Hopson been having an intimate relationship?"

The question had him sitting back down and looking around the room. His first reaction was to question how she knew, but he already knew the answer. His tears and outburst had been enough. There was no point in trying to hide it now. She was gone. Her husband now knew, and that was why she was gone. "She started working here three years ago. She is, I mean was the most amazing woman I have ever met. For me, I knew right away that I loved her. It took her more time to realize we belonged together. We first became intimate about two years ago. It wasn't some torrid affair. We were in love. Her husband is inattentive and cruel. He didn't love her. He could never love her the way I love her, and she would never love him the way she loves me. And for that reason, he took her from me. I know he did this. No on else in the world could ever harm such a kind and perfect creature. She was my soul mate." He sobbed the last word out and then lost it again.

Amy grabbed him a cup of water from the dispenser and offered it to calm him as much as take his mind off of crying. It didn't work very well, but he was a little steadier.

"I am going to have an officer take you home. Please don't leave the city, as I may have further questions for you."

After an officer had escorted him out, Amy looked at Sarah. "Is he a suspect?"

"I think the husband is our best angle, but you never know."

Amy grabbed her notebook and skimmed over her notes. "The husband is Wayne Hopson. Forty-four, married fifteen years, no children, and currently unemployed. He has one arrest for domestic violence against his wife, ten years ago, and nothing since then. No one answered at their residence, but with the domestic violence charge, we should be able to push a warrant through once we get an ID from the doc."

"Not much more we can do here without knowing who the victim is. Let's let the techs do all of their work and see what progress they make." Sarah and Amy headed back out to the car and avoided making eye contact with any of the dozen reporters that had shown up.

"I know this sounds so wrong, but I am starving."

Amy made a disgusted face in response, "I don't think I will eat for the rest of the day."

An hour later, they were back at the station. Sarah had gotten her way, which is how it always went, and they stopped for burgers. They ate outside at the little stand, before heading back to the station. At the station, they ran into Detective Bell on the way to the elevator. He pressed the button on the elevator and stepped back when the doors opened. "Ladies," he said as he ushered them in.

Wanting to give Amy a chance to converse without stuttering, and in an effort to avoid the sexual tension, Sarah stepped out. "I forgot something in the car. Meet me in my office in five minutes Jones."

"Uh, yes ma'am," she said with the look of horror as the elevator doors closed. Sarah figured she would be less nervous without her superior around, but the deer caught in the headlights look had Sarah feeling bad for her now. Had she just bailed from a sinking ship?

By the squealing noises Amy was making when she entered the office, it must have gone well. "I have a date tonight. I have a real date. I haven't been on a date in like a year. Oh crap, what do I wear? You have great clothes that Wes is always buying you. Can I come over and borrow something?"

"Are you saying the only clothes I have worth borrowing are the ones that a man bought for me?" Waiving Amy's concern away, she continued, "I am only kidding. Come over after shift. My whole closet is at your disposal Ms. Jones." Amy gleefully walked out of the office as Sarah's phone rang; she answered it and listened for a minute to the information before hanging up. She walked into the bullpen. "The warrant came through on the Hopson residence, so let's move out."

Thirty minutes later, which would have easily only been fifteen, had there not been two cab drivers fighting in the street, they finally arrived at the Hopson residence. They lived in a very upscale high-rise condo in the middle of the city. Sarah pulled up to the curb and turned on her on-duty lights. The doorman greeted them with a smile and escorted them into the front desk lobby. A tall, beautiful brunette greeted them with a smile, but before she could speak, Sarah had her badge out. "We are serving a warrant at the Hopson residence and want to keep it as quiet as possible. Can you do that?"

"Yes, of course ma'am. Go right on up, they live in 12A. You just take the elevator to the 12th floor and head left; it will be the third unit on the right. Have a nice day."

They entered the elevator and headed to the 12th floor. Sarah knocked on the door of unit 1205, which was the residence Cynthia and Wayne Hopson owned for the past three years of their marriage. When there was no answer, Sarah knocked harder. "Mr. Hopson. This is the New York City Police. We have a warrant and are authorized to enter the premises with the use of force. We will use force if necessary."

They sat and listened for movement from the other side of the door, but heard none. "Last chance Mr. Hopson. We are coming in."

Sarah and Amy drew their weapons and prepared themselves to enter. Sarah kicked the door in and went high while Amy went low. As soon as they entered, they knew why no one had answered the door. In the middle of the living room, hanging from the ceiling fan, was Wayne Hopson. Amy cleared the rest of the unit and saw what she missed at first glance. Sitting in a fruit bowl was a human head. Sarah knew, even without an ID, that it belonged to Cynthia Hopson. On the forehead, written in what looked like a sharpie, was the word whore. Shoved into the left eye socket was a woman's gold and diamond wedding band. In the right socket was a man's gold wedding band.

"It appears Mr. Hopson found out about his wife's affair. I don't think he handled it well. Amy, call in the techs. This is a crime scene. I bet we match this head to the body we found this morning."

"Should someone let Mr. Blake know?"

"He already knew. I don't think he was holding any hope out, but you can confirm it if you think it will give him closure."

Finish up the scene here. I am going to head back and try to close the case up before the end of our shift. I would say this was a straightforward murder-suicide. See you at my place later."

"Thanks Lieutenant."

Chapter 11

Sarah had finished up her paperwork from the day's murder-suicide and was heading home when Wes called.

"Hello beautiful," came out from the other end of the line, as Sarah picked up the phone.

"Hello as well," she replied, happy to hear his voice after such a long day.

"Was it a tough day?" he asked, judging the tone in her voice.

"You could say that. It started with a murder and ended with a suicide. So, just a typical day," she said, sarcastically. "I'm really hoping you can come by tonight," she added in.

"That's actually what I was calling about. I still have so much to do to prepare for my meeting with Senator Kline, that I won't be able to make it by tonight."

Trying not to let her disappointment come through on the phone, she frowned to herself and replied, "That's okay, I know how busy you are and how important this is." As she pulled into her driveway, she saw his car parked along the curb and then saw him sitting on her swing on her front porch. "It's okay, I just got home and my Tuesday night lay is here so it's better that you don't come by," she said, in a devilish voice. "You're a little shit," he quipped back.

Sarah climbed out of the car as she hung up and approached him on the front porch.

"I said I had too much to do tonight, but I managed to squeeze in a little break for my main girl right now." He squeezed her butt and planted a long, passionate kiss on her lips. "I missed you."

"Shhh. Don't tell me, show me, just how much you have missed me."

They were tearing at each other's clothes before the front door was fully closed.

After the day she had, Sarah was feeling like shaking things up a bit. She grabbed Wes by his arm and pushed him back hard onto the sofa. He looked at her with wide eyes as she grabbed his jaw roughly and shoved her tongue in his mouth. He gladly reciprocated, and intertwined his tongue with hers. He went to grab her by the waist, when she slapped his hand. "No, I'm in control tonight," she said, in a naughty voice. She teasingly slid down between his legs onto her knees on the floor in front of him and began to unbutton his pants. She pulled each pant leg off, exposing how ready he was to go. She took him into the palm of her hand and gently caressed him. She slowly worked her way down his chest, and replaced her hand with her mouth. After a few moments, she looked up to see Wes' facial expression, and he begged her for more.

She took all of him in her mouth, feeling it hit in the back of her throat. She continued to please him with a sense of urgency that drove him wild. When Wes professed he couldn't stand it any longer, he begged to be inside of her. She smiled, enjoying a job well done. He moaned out in pleasure as she moved against him, arching and leaning her back against his chest. He reached his arms around her, and cupped both breasts in his hands, giving them a small squeeze. She responded to his hot touch by moving back and forth, faster and faster, until they reached their climax together.

She fell backward and lazily lay on his chest while attempting to catch her breath. "Thanks for the workout Mr. Porter. I had more energy than I realized. That energy really needed to be released, and I can't think of a better way," she managed out, between breaths.

"You know I always enjoy helping out when I can," he replied with a laugh.

"Do you really have to get back to work?" she asked, not wanting him to leave.

"Yes, my love, I do. I have a lot of work left at the office tonight and then I will spend the rest of the night at home, prepping for another exhausting day tomorrow." He playfully picked her up off of his lap and set her on the couch beside him. He leaned in and gave her a long kiss on the lips. He stood up, staring at her perfectly naked body, while he got dressed. He bent down and gently kissed her on the forehead. "I'll call you in the morning beautiful," he said, and walked out the door.

"Looking forward to it," she responded as she closed the door behind him.

Knowing Amy would be by soon, Sarah got dressed and poured a glass of chardonnay. She had closed a case, had mind-blowing sex, and was helping a friend out with a special date. It had turned out to be an okay day. She was contemplating what to do with her night, when there was a knock at the door.

Sarah walked over to open it, as Amy bounded in. "I am so excited, but I am so nervous. I think I might puke," she blurted out, as she strode in past Sarah.

"Well hello to you, Ms. Jones "

"Oh come on, I don't have time for politeness. I have to get sexy, fast. My date is in 45 minutes," she yelled out, already heading down the hall to Sarah's room. Sarah could see her throwing clothes on the bed and on the floor. She had no idea what look Amy was going for, so she didn't even try to help. Sarah drank her wine and tried not to revel too much in watching Amy in a panic.

After 20 minutes of rummaging through the closet and trying on six different outfits, Amy finally decided on the perfect one to wear. She had torn through the closet like a tornado, leaving clothes all over the room. Amy looked around, "shit," she yelled.

Sarah knew her well enough to know what she was concerned about.

"No worries Amy, I can get it all put away," Sarah said, comfortingly.

"Thanks, you're the best," she said as she hugged her and kissed her on the cheek. She bounded down the hall and toward the door as fast as she had come in. "I will give you all the juicy details tomorrow," she said on her way out.

Sarah closed the door and looked around her quiet house. She wondered, what to do tonight?

Chapter 12

Surprising, even herself, Amy was only 15 minutes late. She was still trying to fight off the butterflies in her stomach as she walked up to the front of the restaurant to meet Aaron. He had been a gentleman and offered to pick her up, but she had graciously declined. She never had men at her place on a first date, regardless of whether or not they were a cop. Men tended to think with the part in their pants as opposed to their heads, and to avoid an awkward moment of whether or not to invite him over at the end of the night, it was simply easier to meet him at the restaurant.

Tonight, she had decided to wear her hair up in curls, leaving small pieces sweeping along her face. A beautiful, natural bronze make-up complimented her face and skin tone, and it also matched her outfit perfectly. It had taken much debate, but she felt she had picked the perfect first date attire. She wore a pair of cream-colored flowing pants that contoured her butt just right, along with a tan colored silk shirt that lay open just enough to see a bit of her cleavage. She covered the shirt with a brown lace overlay, and picked a nice pair of suede, tan heels to pull it all together nicely. She wasn't very fond of heels, but Aaron was much taller than she was. The shoes were a nice tan with a dark brown stiletto heel that should have been illegal, as it could be used as a weapon. If she got annoyed with the date, she could just stab him with it. Of course, that was only if she didn't kill herself walking in them first.

She was so nervous she couldn't even remember the name of the restaurant. She just knew it was some French place that she couldn't pronounce. As she approached the door, she saw Aaron standing outside waiting for her, and they locked eyes. She felt her insides flutter with butterflies of excitement, but also fear. She was afraid she might not be able to speak. His devilishly handsome smile had her feeling weak in the knees. He was wearing black dress pants and a stunning blue shirt. To keep it less formal, he went without a tie and jacket. He looked sensational, she thought to herself.

"Wow, you look absolutely stunning Amy," he said, as he reached for her hand and brought it to his lips. He gently brushed his lips across her knuckles with a polite kiss that had her turning to mush. "Shall we?" he said, as he looped his arm through hers and escorted her to their table.

Right away, Amy ordered herself a glass of wine to help loosen herself up and avoid stuttering or rambling like a fool. She found out, over the first drink and appetizer, that they had a lot in common. It made her feel less tense to realize that they were already hitting it off so well. They talked about their childhood growing up, and what drove them to want to be cops. She realized how easy it was for her to talk to him. This suddenly made her nervous again, as it had been a long time since she met someone she connected with. She was hoping that he was feeling the same connection, and by the amount of attention he was paying to her, she assumed he did.

He reached across the table and intertwined his fingers in hers. "I hope this isn't too forward, but I am so happy you agreed to have dinner with me. You seem like such an amazing woman and I feel like we have a lot in common."

"I have my moments," she said jokingly, happy to know he felt the same way.

"See, that's what I mean. You have such drive and determination, but at the same time, you're so fun and easy going."

This had her blushing, and she didn't quite know what to say, but was saved by the server setting the entrées down on the table. She ordered another glass of wine with her dinner, hoping this one would finally drown the last of the butterflies in her stomach. Aaron and Amy chatted and laughed all through dinner. Amy couldn't remember the last time she had felt so comfortable with someone.

After dinner they playfully argued about what dessert to order. A couple moments of witty banter passed, and they finally agreed to share a piece of red velvet cheesecake, along with a bottle of champagne. They fed each other bites, and when it was finished, decided to take the remainder of the champagne to the lovely outdoor patio. The ambiance outside was romantic, as little white lights that looked like stars surrounded them. There were several tables with their own private couches and personal heaters. They chose one in a private corner and got comfortable. She hadn't realized she had been touching his leg until she went to move her hand. Before she could, he set his hand on top of hers. With the other, he lightly cupped her chin and stared into her eyes. She wasn't sure who leaned in first, but she could feel her insides melt at the passion of the kiss. She went wild at the feel of his lips, and the taste of his tongue.

When the kiss was over, Aaron said, "Do you want to go to my place? We can be somewhere more comfortable." Realizing he sounded presumptuous and possibly rude, he tried to correct himself. "I didn't mean for it to sound like that. I just meant if you want to come over, I am not expecting anything from you."

Amy was already standing up with her hand out, waiting for his. "Yes, let's go." She was anxious to kiss him again and wanted her hands all over his perfectly sculpted body.

"I'll get us a cab," he said, as they walked out of the restaurant and hailed down a cab. In the back seat, they sat with their hands locked into one another's.

She wanted him so badly that she could almost taste it. She didn't normally go home with a guy so quickly, but she couldn't ignore the spark she felt with him. There was a chemistry she had never experienced before. When she leaned over to kiss him again, she ran her hand up his leg and found that he was just as ready as she was, and very well endowed. His pants were so tight against him; she thought the zipper might pop. She could think of nothing else, but putting her hands all over his body. Luckily, before she could embarrass herself and put on a show for the cab driver, they came to a stop. They had pulled in front of a small, quaint house, about five blocks from Sarah's. She had been so engrossed in him that she hadn't even paid attention to where they were going.

He fumbled with the keys in the front door, while Amy made her way into his pants. She freed his erection and caressed him with her hands. As the door opened, they shuffled over the threshold, Amy never letting him go. He slammed the door shut behind them, and then fumbled with the lock before walking her into his living room. They continued to kiss and pet each other all over, like a couple of horny teenagers, when Aaron abruptly stopped Amy's wandering hand and pulled back from her kiss. Amy must have had a bewildered look on her face as Aaron began talking before she could even get a word out.

"I know we have been going all hot and heavy but I have to put on the brakes before I can't control myself any longer."

Amy leaned in toward him and whispered, "Why would you need to control yourself, I am putty in your hand. Do as you may with me."

"As tempting as that may be, I really like you and feel a very deep connection already. The last thing I want to do is take advantage of you after two glasses of wine and half a bottle of champagne," Aaron managed to say, almost not believing he was turning this down.

Amy sat there, a bit confused. On one hand, she was so pleased to hear him speak like such a gentleman, but on the other hand, her body was aching for his touch. She looked at him with puppy dog eyes and pouty lips.

"Are you sure we shouldn't just be naughty?" she whimpered.

"Oh Lord woman, don't make this any harder on me than it already is. I want nothing more than to ravage your hot little body, but tonight isn't the night. I will, however, take you into my bedroom and snuggle you better than anyone has ever done before," he said with a smile.

Amy smiled back at him as she grabbed his hand, "That sounds fantastic, I would love to do that."

They made their way down the hall, towards Aaron's bedroom. Amy was just now able to see how nice and neat he kept his house, as she wasn't glued to his face anymore. They entered into the bedroom, where there was a beautiful cherry pine king size bed, covered with a suede blue comforter and lots of pillows.

"Looks comfy," Amy said, as she got down to her bra and panties and climbed under the covers.

"Ready for some serious snuggling?" Aaron said in a deep, masculine voice as he got down to his boxers and joined her under the covers.

"This is the perfect ending to our perfect night," Amy said as she kissed his lips and laid her head down on his chest.

"Agreed," Aaron replied as he turned off the side table lamp and closed his eyes.

Chapter 13

Lucy sat staring at herself in the mirror. She had tried very hard to convince herself to get ready and get to work, but to no avail. Even her dwindling bank account wasn't motivation enough. She had told herself it was because it was cold, and she was tired, but she knew herself better. She was scared of who she had become the last few times she had worked. She still hadn't put the pieces together to figure out what was going on with her. She had done things she never thought possible of herself. As a young girl, she fantasized about hurting her stepfather, but she had never acted on it, nor did she believe she could. Or could she have? The opportunity had never presented itself, so she couldn't be sure. At one time, she had known the answer. But, she wasn't so sure now.

Her stepfather had been a cruel man. Her mother had married him when Lucy was twelve, and was never happy. He cheated and made her mother cry all the time. She couldn't remember a week that went by that he didn't come home smelling of other women's perfume and lingering sex. He would say cruel things and call her mother horrible names, when she confronted him. He always denied the affairs, but never stopped having them. Lucy remembered the smells distinctly. There was never the same one. She got stuck washing the stench of perfumed sex and lipstick from her stepfather's clothes. Her mother would always say, "I can't handle cleaning the lies off his clothes, do the laundry for me baby." So, Lucy always did as her mother asked. Lucy tried to be a friend to her, since she had no one else. Lucy's mother would wait up for him until all hours of the night, and sob when he didn't come home. The sobbing would turn into drinking, and the drinking would turn into anger. She would shout about how she hated him. She would tell Lucy they were leaving and how she could find a better man. Lucy wondered why her mother had needed a man at all. She just didn't see the point. All he did was cheat on her and verbally abuse her. Why would anyone want that?

Lucy never knew if her mother would have gotten the courage to leave. Ironically, her stepfather got bored and ended up leaving them. On his way out, he had told her of all the women he had been with, and how they never bored him like she had. He told her she wasn't pretty enough to keep his attention, that she was a lousy housewife in public, and a boring housewife in the bedroom. He wanted excitement and was done pretending with her. He had called her a boring, nagging old hag and slammed the door on his way out. Her mother cried for days. She turned to the liquor more and more, and became a recluse, wallowing in her self-pity.

Lucy loved her mom and wanted to be her friend, but dreamed of getting away. She stayed by her mother's side and was a friend to her when she needed it. But, when the time came and she turned eighteen, Lucy left. She felt no guilt and went out to live a life that did not involve men hurting her. She had stayed in contact with her mother, but didn't talk to her as often as she should have. She regretted that sometimes, but never regretted leaving. She couldn't spend her life watching her mother wither away into a bitter, old woman.

The one thing Lucy had learned from her mother was to never let a man break you down or hurt you, and Lucy never would. She lay on the futon and drifted off to sleep, with echoes of her mother's voice swimming in her head.

Chapter 14

It was a rare occurrence, but Sarah was late to work. She drove like a mad woman, trying to get to work, in order to avoid listening to Amy rub it in on how she was always early. To Sarah's surprise, when she pulled into the parking lot, Amy was just getting in as well. She was getting out of a car with Detective Bell. They were laughing and giggling with each other. As soon as they saw Sarah, they came to attention.

"Lieutenant," they said simultaneously, but Amy was having a hard time holding back her smile.

"Whatever it is you two are so damn giddy about, it's probably best you two keep it to yourselves."

"Yes ma'am," Aaron responded, while Amy's face looked doubtful she would be able to keep things to herself. Sarah rolled her eyes at both of them as they all headed for the elevator. She pretended to not notice the quick kiss they shared before the doors opened. She wasn't surprised to see them change as they went through the doors to the bullpen, and quickly returned to professional cop behavior. They had their work faces on and were ready for the day. They both knew better, that if anyone caught on to them, they would be teased relentlessly.

"Get me some coffee and meet me in my office," Sarah told Amy.

"Yes, Lieutenant." Amy pushed her way through all the guys, to the coffee pot. The coffee pot location seemed to attract males gossiping, more often than females. Amy grabbed herself a donut and grabbed one for Sarah. She made her way into Sarah's office and set down the coffee and donuts, anxiously waiting for a chance to brag about her night.

Knowing what Amy wanted, Sarah took a bite of her donut and spent as long as she could, savoring it in order to torture Amy. "Fine, let's hear all about it," Sarah finally said.

Amy told her all about dinner, sparing no details. Sarah thought she seemed like a schoolgirl describing her first crush, but she was happy. She had never seen Amy so happy and lit up. She was glad her friend seemed to be in heaven. She remembered her first date with Wes, and supposed she felt the same way. He still made her nervous and weak in the knees, which she supposed was a good thing, after so many years together.

Amy was getting to the juicy details, when they were interrupted by a knock at the door. A tall, skinny officer popped his head in the door.

"Sorry to interrupt ma'am. Mitchell and Sanchez were headed to a body dump when they got t-boned by a dump truck. Can you pick it up?"

Standing up from her desk, she grabbed her gear. "Have dispatch send all the information to my phone and let them know we are on our way. Thank you officer." Turning to Amy, she said, "Girl gossip hour is over."

"I was just getting to all the dirty details too," Amy said, somewhat sad for the gossip to end so soon.

"I bet you were. I don't think I want to hear the dirty parts or what things you were doing to Detective Bell's dirty parts. I don't want to visualize that every time I see him," Sarah said adamantly.

They got in the elevator, then got out and headed towards the car. They drove towards the crime scene, and with only a bit of traffic, they pulled up roughly twenty minutes later, to a sea of people and yellow tape. It was a small alley behind a large commercial structure that housed a gym, a deli, and an electronics store. The scene had been taped off to keep the reporters away, although they were already hovering like vultures. Sarah loved her job, but some days, she wished humanity would win and she would have nothing to do all day.

That just wasn't the way it was though. There was murder everyday and Sarah would never be out of a job. It was just the way the world worked. It was the way the world had ended for the guy lifelessly leaning up against the dumpster.

"No blood found on scene, and from the looks of it, this guy bled out from the femoral artery." Molly was on shift again, and gave Sarah a quick nod. "This slice through his thigh would have opened him up and he would have bled out in a matter of minutes, if not seconds. There is no way he was killed here. There isn't even a blood trail. That means his heart stopped beating long before he made it here."

"Do we have an ID?" Sarah asked.

Molly looked around for the crime scene technicians. "Yeah, that small blonde kid over there found and bagged his wallet. He's got an ID for you." Molly moved back over the body as Sarah stepped away. "Oh, and Lieutenant, body temp puts his time of death in the early morning hours; sometime between one and five I would say. Just enough time to dump him before it got light out."

"This area is well known for prostitution," Amy pointed out. "Do you think this is another victim of the Sex Slayer?"

"What the hell is the Sex Slayer?"

"It's the name I have given the prostitute that's killing these guys. I think it's catchy. It has a nice ring to it."

"I am contemplating sending you for a psych eval Amy. You have some serious issues."

Amy stifled a little giggle and retrieved the ID that had been collected. "Martin James, forty-eight, and an organ donor. His license says he is from Manhattan. There's no money and no credit cards in here. If it was a robbery, why not just take the whole wallet?"

"That's what we need to figure out. He may have been robed, but something else went down as well, that got him killed. Get me next of kin, and the surveillance videos from the stores around here that have cameras. Let's see if anyone saw who dropped Mr. James off here. If it was our woman, then she had some help. That guy looks to be about 200 pounds. That's a lot of deadweight to handle for a man or woman, but harder for a woman."

"You are good Lieutenant. ID says he weighs 215. I will see if we can spot a vehicle on any of the security discs and just in case, put an order in for traffic cams as well."

"Good idea. I will notify the next of kin and start the report. Let's try to find anyone he knew and get some information on him. Find out what kind of situation he would have been in that ended this way," she said, looking at the lifeless body of Martin James. "Get two or three officers to canvas the area. Have them talk to everyone. Maybe we will get lucky and someone saw or heard something."

It was almost the end of shift, and Sarah wanted nothing more than to get home. She listened to Martin's daughter cry hysterically, for over an hour, and deny that her father was gone. She just kept saying what an amazing man he was, and how no one would ever hurt him. She thought there had been a mistake and that her father was coming home. "You're wrong. I know you are." She kept calling his phone, over and over again. "He will answer. He is going to answer this time," she kept weeping.

It had taken quite a while for Amy to calm the girl down. They convinced her to call her husband at work and have him come home. Watching a grown woman break down like that broke Sarah's heart. She always felt drained and weak after notifying people that their loved ones were gone. They wouldn't come walking in the front door again, or leave some funny message on their cell phone. It was one of the harder parts of the job, but she did it with strength and kindness. After the husband finally arrived home to console his sobbing wife, Amy and Sarah headed back to the station.

They sat, going through the notes and discussing possible scenarios, when Amy got a call on her cell phone. After a couple moments, she hung up and retrieved a scan that had just come through her computer. She quickly walked back into the office to fill Sarah in. "There is one angle of a white van parked in front of the alley." Amy set the picture in front of Sarah. "It doesn't capture the license plate or who is driving, but traffic cams may be able to help. The tapes should be here by morning."

"Not much else we can do here tonight. Call it a day Amy, and head home. There will be plenty more on your plate for tomorrow."

"Perfect. I am ready to get out of here. I am seeing Aaron again tonight. He wants to cook me dinner at his place," she said giddily.

"Good thing he is cooking, and you're not. That would be a good way to make him run away, fast."

"I can't even pretend to be offended. I know how much I suck in the kitchen." Amy grabbed her bag and headed for the door. "You are leaving too, right? Do you get to see that delicious-looking man of yours?"

"You have your own to fantasize about, get that look off your face when you think about Wes," she said laughing. "I'm going to head home in five and Wes is coming over with Chinese. He has a very early start tomorrow, so he wants to stay at his place, but still wants to see me. I think that means I get Chinese food, a quickie, and my bed all to myself. Doesn't get much better than that."

"I still owe you a story full of dirty details. I will wait until tomorrow and have two stories with lots of extra dirty details." Amy waived and walked out. She met Aaron at the elevator and it took everything she had in her to not jump him right there.

"Detective," he said with a wink.

Just the one wink had her melting. She could already feel the butterflies stirring in her stomach, and her whole body was beginning to tingle. What was this man doing to her?

Chapter 15

They rode down the elevator in silence, and almost sprinted to his car. Once in, they looked around for peering eyes and mauled each other like it had been days since they last saw each other. Their lips met with an exploding passion and their mouths fused together in a long, intimate kiss that left them both breathless.

"I have been waiting all day to do that," Aaron confessed when they sat back in their seats. "I couldn't stop thinking about you all day."

"Yeah, I have that effect on men," she giggled out as he teasingly poked her side. "In all seriousness though, I know what you mean. You are quite the distraction."

They drove, holding hands and talking about their day. Once again, they barely got in the front door before they started ripping each other's clothes off. This time, Amy was the one to put the brakes on a little. "What about dinner?" she mumbled out in between kisses as his fingers continued to work on unbuttoning her shirt.

"We are having dessert first," he said as he ripped her shirt open and sent buttons flying everywhere.

"That way, you can still have wine with dinner. If I take advantage of you now, I won't have to worry about stopping like a gentleman later if you have a couple glasses," he said while unbuttoning her pants.

She smiled as she leaned in for more kisses. "I like the way you think," she uttered out while still trying to keep her lips pressed to his. Aaron was now stripping himself down to his boxers when Amy stopped him and said, "Allow me." She got down on her knees and slowly pulled the soft blue cotton boxers down to his ankles, exposing his large, hard manhood. She took it into her hand softly and began to stroke it back and forth. She started to realize that with her small hands and his large size; she may need both hands to fully complete this task properly. As she brought her second hand into play, and was about to put him in her mouth, Aaron stopped her and pulled her back up to eye level. She was a little taken back, when he scooped her up and carried her into the bedroom.

Once there, he laid her softly on the bed and removed her panties. She was quivering with excitement as she felt his hot breath pant against her moistened area. He caressed his tongue slowly back and forth awhile before having his fingers enter her gently. Amy moaned out and arched her back with approval. As he began to increase the speed of his tongue and fingers, Amy felt as though she would burst as she begged him on with breathless pleas of continuance. This only further enticed Aaron to increase the speed and depth of his fingers. Amy cried out in pleasure as she felt herself climax. Aaron couldn't stand it any longer, and mounted himself upon her. With a deep thrust, he entered deep into her. Amy felt as though she would see stars from the amount of pleasure she was feeling in every inch of her being. This man is a god she thought, as she dug her fingers into his back and encouraged him for more. He continued to thrust himself inside of her while leaning above her, looking deep into her eyes. He felt her body tense as she reached her second climax, and he knew it was time for him to release as well.

Together, they finished as they gazed intensely at one another, both realizing the strong feelings that they had already developed for one another. Amy looked at him and said, "Wow." She had a smile that was beaming from ear to ear, and was tingling all over from head to toe. "Hey, that wow goes for you as well. I had great inspiration with that sexy body of yours."

"Well you better get this sexy body fed, I'm starving," Amy said as she slipped her panties back on and climbed into one of his overly large t-shirts that was sitting on the nightstand.

"Looking good in my clothes," Aaron said as he patted her butt on the way to the kitchen.

Chapter 16

Just a few blocks away, Sarah and Wes were sharing Chinese food and discussing their day's work. Wes was telling Sarah about the time crunch he was on and complaining about people not doing their job. "It's been such a long week, but it makes it so much easier getting to see you in the middle of all of it." He rubbed the back of his hand down her soft cheek and placed a gentle kiss on her nose. He reached under her shirt and playfully cupped her breast as if by accident, while he exposed her necklace. "It makes me even happier to see that you wear this. I know it's a bit much for you, but I love that you wear it for me."

"Of course I wear it. It only comes off at night. It's not my style, but it was from you so I absolutely love it. You know everything else comes off at night too."

"Really?" he said, intrigued.

"The shirt comes off first," she said, as she slowly lifted it over her head and tossed it on the floor.

Wes reached up and skimmed a finger over her bra and down to her belly button. "What's next?"

"Then I take my pants off," she said as she slowly unzipped her jeans and stepped out of them, leaving her standing in front of him in her matching black lace bra and thong.

He reached around and ran his hands along her buttocks and hungrily looked up at her. "It all comes off?"

She unhooked her bra and let it fall to the floor, exposing her perky breasts. Her nipples were hard with excitement and her breath hitched as Wes ran his thumb along one of them. She then slid her panties down to her ankles and stepped out of them. She sat, straddling his fully clothed body. "All of it," she whispered into his ear before giving it a quick nip. He wrapped his hand around the back of her neck and drew her in for a deep kiss.

"You are a naughty little thing tonight, aren't you?" he said, while gripping her bare ass cheeks in his hands.

She could feel him growing beneath her as she sat on top of his erection, wanting nothing more than to feel him enter her. She began to grind on him, whimpering in his ear, "I want it, and I want it now."

He was more than happy to oblige her demands. He picked her up and threw her onto her back. He stood above her and stripped down to nothing but his sexy bare body. She looked up at him with a devilish grin as he pulled her legs apart wide and slid himself inside of her. For an earth-shattering fifteen minutes, he thrust himself in and out of her as she pulled him in deeper and deeper. They came together and lay in each other's arms for a short minute.

"I wish I didn't have to leave so quickly." He apologized for having to head out, while he dressed and promised next time he would stay and cuddle her all night.

She put her robe on as he went to grab her for a kiss. She kissed him back and told him she understood. She walked him to the door and gave him one last squeeze as she locked the door behind him and thought to herself, another night alone.

Chapter 17

It was another night that Lucy had to force herself to work. Things had changed so rapidly that she wasn't sure who she was when she became Lucy Lust. It didn't matter tonight which persona she was; she was broke. She desperately needed to make some fast money. Her bills were paid, but her savings had dwindled down because she had played hooky from hooking for a couple nights. She liked having a small chunk in savings for an emergency. You just never knew what could happen.

She sat at her vanity like so many nights before, but tonight, something was different. She looked different; her reflection was nothing but Lucy Lust tonight. She saw no part of her real self in the person staring back at her. Tonight, her hair was long and blonde. The wig was a platinum color, full of long, soft curls. She put one long blue extension on the front to add some excitement. Her contacts were the same shade of blue as the feathery highlights she had added in her hair. She touched up her light blue shadow and eyeliner after putting her fake eyelashes on. They were her extra long and thick lashes. She felt they hid what truly lies beneath her eyes.

Tonight she chose a simple outfit: black leather pants, a long-sleeved black lace top that exposed her flat stomach, and matching black heels. She wanted to be in sweat pants, a sweatshirt and slippers, but she didn't think she would get much business that way. It was almost 11 o'clock when she walked outside into the brisk New York night. She was getting a later start than she had wanted, but she was proud of herself for even getting her butt out the door at all. She walked two blocks, trying to avoid her usual spots. She didn't want to see any of the other girls or be seen. She picked a spot near a seedy motel and walked around until a car pulled up, signaling her over.

The Jeep that was stopped had five young men crammed in. The driver, who barely looked fifteen, spoke first, "It's my boy's 21st birthday. We want to give him something real nice."

The boy in the back that was pointed to blushed when Lucy looked at him. When she smiled at him, all the boys started shouting and urging him to get out of the car. The driver was yelling at all his friends to hand over their money.

"So we each chipped in and want you to give him whatever $500 can get." The driver handed her the money and winked at his friend. A chant of "Ryan, Ryan, Ryan," had began.

"Ryan, I am guessing it is." When the young man nodded, she had him walk with her towards the motel. "Well, Ryan," handing him some of the money back, "Go get us a room and meet me at the ice machine right over there." She walked to the ice machine and imagined the poor boy was having a heart attack, while trying to get the room by himself. He seemed more scared than excited. He came walking up with a key and handed it to her. "How old are you really, Ryan?"

As they rounded the corner and stuck the key into room 12, he answered, "Nineteen."

"No reason to be so nervous. I am just a girl and you are just a guy." A guy, young enough for this to be wrong, she thought. But, she needed the money, so she would do what she needed to do. She shut the door behind them and closed the blinds. She sat down on the bed and patted the spot beside her, inviting him to come sit. "Calm down, and breathe; this is supposed to be enjoyable. Have you thought about what you want?"

"No, not really. I have only been with one girl," he said sheepishly. "She just broke up with me last week and that's why the guys thought this was a good idea."

"You don't seem to agree with your friends."

"Don't get me wrong, you are hot and I would love to be with you. But, I just don't think I can do it. You know, like he can't do it," he said, looking down at his lap.

"I get it. I am a great listener. Why don't we just talk about whatever you want to talk about until you feel comfortable and ready."

His body relaxed and he smiled at her. "I would like that." An hour passed, and they were still talking. He had opened up quite a bit, and told her all about his school and why the girl of his dreams had broken his heart. Lucy actually liked how sweet and innocent he was. It was rare to see a teenage boy that genuine. He stood up and grabbed her off the bed and embraced her in a big bear hug. "Thank you so much. I bet you are well worth the money, but I really enjoyed the last hour the way it was. I will tell all my friends they got their money's worth."

She looked at him, a little surprised, but wasn't going to argue with free money. "If you are sure?"

"I am. Thank you again, and have a nice night," he said with a genuine smile as he walked out the door.

Lucy couldn't remember ever making such an easy $500. Not only was she pleased with the easy money, but also ecstatic she wouldn't have to feel guilt after being with such a young boy. She knew they were men, just like the rest of them, but she tried to stay away from young clients. Most of her established clients traveled for the holidays and away from the cold. They would return closer to the spring, so she would have to make due with whoever else was out looking on this chilly night.

Ryan had returned the key to the front desk for her, so she began to walk towards the street again. Before she made it around the corner, one of the motel room doors opened. A tall, thin, balding man stepped out. "You do rooms by the hour?" he asked Lucy, staring her up and down.

He was an average looking man, nothing extraordinary about him. He could have been handsome, had he not let the hairline recede back to the point of balding. "I do, for the right price," she replied, noticing the gold band circling his left ring finger. She felt a spike of anger as she wondered if this was what her stepfather was out doing each night she had to watch her mother stare out the window, crying and waiting for him to come home. She let the anger pass and shot him a sexy smile that said she was worth every penny.

"I think we can work something out." He smiled at her and gestured her into the room as he looked around before closing the door.

Never leaving her back to a John, she turned around and did a sexy saunter into the room. "What were you thinking baby? What can I do for you?"

"There are so many things I want," he said, licking his lips. "I want to do all the things to you my boring wife never let me do."

She felt the anger stirring again and wondered what made this guy any different from her stepfather. Did he honestly not look in the mirror and think he was the problem? Maybe his wife wouldn't be boring if he hadn't let his hair fall out and his body fall apart. Lucy could only imagine how bored his wife probably was with him, yet she probably isn't throwing out their vows for a quick roll in the sheets. He laid a couple one hundred dollar bills on the nightstand, and she plastered on a smile.

"I want to watch first. Just slowly take your clothes off, and let me watch." He was practically drooling as she stripped the leather pants off and threw them on the chair. His eyes got wide as she took off her shirt and bra, exposing her breasts. He walked over and cupped both breasts in his hands before leaning down to lick each nipple. She moved to take her panties off, and he stopped her. "I want to," he said as he laid her down on the bed and pulled her thong down her legs and over her feet before throwing them on the floor. He stood above her, staring for a minute. "You are so much more beautiful than she is. You see this," he said, freeing his erection. "She can't do that for me anymore. But you, without you even touching me I am ready for you. Are you ready for me?"

Not in this lifetime buddy. "Oh, I am ready baby, get over here," she said, wondering if her teeth were actually clenched like she felt they were. He undressed and moved above her. He rapidly caressed her breasts and licked her nipples. He was panting and making sounds like a wounded animal before he was even inside her. He used his tongue to moisten her between her thighs, and then entered her. He only moved in and out twice before he had to stop.

No wonder his wife didn't give it up to him. Lucy was being paid to enjoy it, and was having a hard time pretending. She imagined this being comparable to mating with a baboon. His huffing and puffing were creeping her out, even considering she should be used to this in her line of work. He stopped a second to take off his wedding ring. Finally, he was going to show his wife a little respect.

Oh, how Lucy was mistaken.

He placed the ring on his right index finger and slid it and two other fingers inside her. His face was covered with excitement and joy. "I will show that worthless bitch to say no to me. You say no to me and look what I get to do."

Lucy immediately went back in time, thinking of her mother crying after her stepfather came home smelling of Jasmine and sex. He screamed at her that she was worthless and he would find someone who wanted to be what he needed. Quickly coming back to the present, Lucy snapped. Before she could even stop herself, she had her foot planted in his gut and used the bed as leverage to kick him across the room. His body looked like a rag doll as he flew into the corner table. His face was a morph between shock and anger.

"What the hell was that for?" He stood up, looking in the mirror at the cut in his back. He walked up to her and smiled, "You may be a shit ton hotter than my wife, but you sure have crazy down like she does."

Lucy punched him square in the face and his nose started to bleed. His face was distorted with blood and utter shock. She couldn't stop herself, and before she knew it, she was on top of him, straddling his naked body while pounding on his face. She stopped when her knuckles hurt and realized he wasn't moving. You couldn't see his face through all the blood smeared on it. But, she saw a face when she looked at him. She saw her stepfather. Anger and rage were brewing inside of her.

There was no sense of right and wrong. She was being completely controlled by emotion. The emotion had her grabbing the small knife she had for protection out of her purse. She straddled him again, knife in the air above her head. She hesitated, staring at him. When his eyes opened wide with surprise, she came down hard with the knife into his chest. She aimed for his heart and that was exactly where she landed. He lay beneath her, bleeding to death all over the motel carpet. Now, he could never hurt her mother again.

She could hear nothing over the sound of her heart pounding and her lungs trying to catch any air it could. She felt light-headed and dizzy as she scrambled back to sit against the bed. She stared at his bloody, naked body and felt empty inside. Why couldn't Lucy control herself? She shook her head and reminded herself it wasn't Lucy that couldn't keep control. She knew that she was the one that would pay the price if she got caught in this room with a bloody body. She quickly got dressed and threw the sheets in the bathtub. She put on a shower cap over her wig and took all the soap she could find. She scrubbed down his naked body and removed any part of her that could be on him. She then covered him with a towel and wiped the rest of the room for fingerprints with the other towel. She covered the sheets with bubble bath, shampoo, and conditioner before letting scalding hot water run on them. She was pretty sure there would be no fluids from her on the sheets, but she had to be sure. She cleaned the blood off of her knife and put it back in her purse. She looked around one last time, and when she was confident that no trace of her would be found in the room, she opened the door slightly. Seeing no one around, she walked out and around the back of the building, towards her studio. Taking a five-block detour to ensure she wasn't being followed, she arrived at her studio 30 minutes later. It was late. She was cold and shaken to the core. She wanted nothing more than to get out of the clothes she was in, get to her own bed, and sleep the nightmares away. Another night of asking herself, *what the hell happened*?

Chapter 18

"Sex Slayer strikes again! I told you it was catchy, Lieutenant." Amy sat in the car anxiously as they drove to the scene. Another murder has occurred. This time, it happened in a motel known for catering to prostitutes and their Johns. Since Sarah had been involved in the last cases, her commander wanted her on this one too.

"When we get to the crime scene, please try to act a little less excited about a murder, Detective."

Amy frowned at her. "Well, we are a little moody this morning. I saw on the local news channel online that they used my catch line. They actually referred to her as the Sex Slayer." She looked away from Sarah, back out the window, "And I am not excited about murder, I just had a good night. A really good night."

"I am happy for you, but the juicy details will have to wait until later." Sarah put on her on-duty light and parked in front of the Comfy View Inn. She wondered what view they were referring to and what part of this place looked comfy. "By the way, we got a lead on the van that was seen outside the alley where Martin James' body was found. Traffic Division sent me over info this morning. Known drug dealers, so it should prove to be an interesting conversation. We will head over after we wrap up here and see what information we can find."

It wasn't hard to miss an FBI agent in a crowd. None of the cops, higher rank or not, wore suits in the field. Sarah recognized him as a federal agent immediately. He was tall and beautiful. That was the only word that came to mind. He was easily around 6'2" and he was solid. Even under the suit, you could see the lines of his muscles and the way his shirt gripped his chest. His sandy blonde hair was cut short, but still had enough length to not be a buzz cut. His eyes were crystal blue. Not the deep blue that Wes was gifted with, but a sparkling blue that made you think of water, yet dried your mouth out at the same time. She could hear Amy mumbling behind her, saying he looked good enough to eat. Sarah wanted to tell her to shut up, but she couldn't argue with her.

Gathering herself, she walked right up to him with her hands on her hips, "And just what the hell are the feds doing at my crime scene?"

He turned slowly, taking her in, "Well I would assume you know who I am. And you are?"

"I am taking my crime scene back. There is no need for the FBI here.

"Actually," he paused for a moment, waiting for her to give her rank and name. When she just stood there staring at him, he smiled and went on, "You have two dead that were presumed to be with a prostitute at the time of death, and another man claiming he was attacked by a prostitute. This makes body number three. And since you haven't been in the room yet to see that he was naked and rented this room for three hours, I will forgive the attitude. The FBI sent me to investigate these deaths and make sure there is not a prostitute out there killing her Johns. If it turns out there is, there is going to be more of me. You may want to work with me so you can get me out of your hair faster."

"That idea works for me. Now, who the hell are you?"

"Special Agent Travis Stone," he said while meeting her gaze and grabbing her hand.

When he shook her hand, he held it for a couple seconds longer than needed. Making her nervous, she pulled her hand back and gestured at Amy, "This is my partner Detective Jones, and I am Lieutenant Sarah Carmichael. And this is my scene."

"Yes it is. I am just here to observe and gather information. But, should it come down to it, I will make this visit official instead of informational." He gestured toward the hotel room and smiled when she glared at him, "After you Lieutenant."

"This is such bullshit," she grumbled under her breath as she stormed off toward the hotel room.

"Yeah, but he is hot," Amy whispered as she caught up. "Like the kind of hot that has you wanting to tear his clothes off in front of these people. Oh, like Wes hot." Getting an icy glare from Sarah, she said, "I was just pointing it out and did you see the way he looked at you?"

"All I can see is that this guy is going to be a pain in my ass."

Standing behind Sarah and Amy, Travis surveyed the scene again. "The scene is completely wiped clean. The techs couldn't even pull the victim's prints from anywhere in the room. Minus the body and blood, this room shows no sign of anyone even being in here. It's just as neat as the scene at the Millennium Hilton."

"That's why you are here? You think this perp is too smart for the NYPD?" Covering her shoes with crime scene booties provided, Sarah moved around the room, gathering what information she could.

"Not at all Lieutenant. I am just saying our girl, whoever she is, is good. She is very good at making herself invisible. I don't know about you, but finding the invisible is not a skill set I have mastered yet."

"Sarcasm sure is though, Agent Stone." Sarah could feel his eyes on her and met his stare. "That's something you have down pat, it seems."

Now smiling, "As I can see, politeness and charm are two skill sets you have mastered," he replied. "Now that the pleasantries are concluded, I need to go over the case files."

"I am not handing over my case files to you," Sarah snapped out.

"Fine, we can go over them together. I have reserved conference room three for the week. Meet me there at nineteen hundred. You bring the case files, and I will bring burgers and fries."

"I have a lead on another case. I have people I need to question downtown. I may not make it back to the station in time."

Enjoying the tension more than she would admit, Amy stepped between the two, "I can go question the Rodriguez brothers, Lieutenant. I will report back to you at the station." Turning to Travis, she added, "I like my burgers well-done with curly fries."

"Detective Jones, these men are known drug dealers and have no qualms about hurting cops or women. Take an officer or two with you."

"Yes, ma'am. I will meet you at the station at nineteen hundred." Amy turned and headed to gather up two officers. She didn't feel she needed to be protected, but after all, she didn't have a vehicle. She had driven with Sarah, and judging by her mood, asking Sarah to get a ride with Travis Stone would be a bad idea.

"I like her," Travis said, watching her get in the car. "She is efficient and tough, but you can tell she is also sweet. You agree I can see. You two are friends outside of work. That was easy enough to see."

"She is seeing someone so try to keep your panties on." Sarah continued to take notes and headed toward the door.

"I like her, but she's not my type. I go for the overwhelmingly strong, stubborn, bullheaded type," he said, staring at Sarah. He sent her a wicked little grin, "they tend to be more fun and keep you on your toes all the time. I like the challenge."

"I see you more as going for the girl who is intellectually, let's say, challenged," she said, mocking his words. "That way she makes you look better."

Travis stepped in front of Sarah and placed his arm against the wall next to her head. He got within inches from her face and she could feel his breath on her and smell his cologne. "I think you would be very surprised to find out what I go for, Lieutenant."

Being tongue-tied was not something that happened to Sarah often, and she wasn't sure how to handle it. Her hands were getting clammy and her head fuzzy. She was sure he could hear her heart pounding against her chest. She had butterflies in her stomach, but they weren't fluttering, they were slamming against her insides, fighting to be released. She was not going to let this arrogant man see that he was getting to her.

She put a finger in his chest and backed him up. "Don't get in my space like that. I have a report to write and a medical examiner to harass. I will have your case files for you at nineteen hundred. Excuse me," she said, walking around him back to her vehicle.

Travis stood there, watching her leave. He wasn't sure if he had gotten to her or not, but he knew she had gotten to him from the second he saw her. He could still feel the stirring all over his body. She had a presence unlike any woman he had ever met before. Actually, unlike any person he had met before. She commanded attention with one look, and was very capable of handling it when she got it. He knew she was an excellent cop from reading her file, but he wanted to know her as more than a cop. He wondered what kind of woman she was, off of the job. Their little encounter had him wanting more time with her. She was going to keep him on his toes.

Amy and the two officers, Perkins and Dillon, pulled up in front of the last known address for the Rodriguez brothers. The van that had been seen on security and traffic cams came back registered to the older of the two, Jorge Rodriguez. He had a long rap sheet, including several drug charges and theft. His younger brother, Raul Rodriguez, had a more physical history. In the three years since his eighteenth birthday, he had four charges of assault and a murder charge that was dropped due to the disappearance of all witnesses.

Perkins put the car in park in front of the building and watched people scatter like rats. "Detective, they are both sitting on the stoop, about two buildings down."

"Ok, get out of the car." The three of them stepped out of the vehicle and heard someone shout, "Fuck off pigs," from down the street. "Jorge and Raul," she said as she walked towards them. "I just have some quick simple questions to ask you, but please show me your hands for my own peace of mind."

Both men stood up and took off running. Jorge turned around and opened fire as he ran. Amy shoved Officer Perkins out of the way of one of the bullets and sent him flying into a parked car. Officer Dillon caught up with Raul and knocked him to the ground. They both lost their weapons in the fall, and Raul managed a good kick to Officer Dillon's head. "Officer Perkins, get your ass up and get that asshole that shot at us," Amy shouted as she went to aide Officer Dillon.

Officer Dillon fought to keep his hand up and avoid kicks to the head, but Raul kept kicking him everywhere he could. As Officer Dillon slipped into blackness, Amy was there, slamming Raul to the ground.

Amy hit him dead center on his body, and sent them both flying. She was on top of him, pulling her weapon out when he punched her in the jaw. She felt the inside of her skull rattle and fought to keep her vision straight. She was on her back now, and he was kicking her repeatedly. She could hear the cracking of things breaking inside of her, but she managed to get her foot out and land a kick to his groin. He squealed and stumbled back, but recovered too quickly. Amy knew he was on a methamphetamine and this was a severely unfair fight. She scrambled to her feet in time for his kick to miss her face, but it landed square on her chest and she staggered back, gasping for air. Keeping her weapon out of his reach, she pivoted, but not in time to get her weapon out. He grabbed her by the hair and slammed her down, face first into the bricks on the building wall. She heard shouts and screaming as she struggled to keep her balance. He shoved her and took off running. As she fell to her knees, Amy opened her eyes as wide as she could and pointed her weapon.

"Stop Raul!" she shouted. "I will shoot you." She pulled the trigger, right before she collapsed and let the pain take her into the darkness that had crept in over her mind.

Chapter 19

Sarah was heading back to the station when she got the call about Amy. She raced to the hospital and almost strangled the nurse who told her she couldn't go in and see her.

"She's in surgery, ma'am."

"Do I look like a ma'am to you?" she shouted. "Lieutenant. I am a lieutenant with the NYPD and my partner is back there."

The nurse understood her emotion and tried to calm her down. "I understand how you feel Lieutenant, but Ms. Jones is in surgery and there is nothing you can do for her right now. As soon as we have information, you will get it. Now, please go have a seat and try to calm down."

"Calm down. Right," she said to herself as she walked towards the waiting area. She spotted the two officers that Amy had left with and felt pleased to have people to take her anger out on. "You two," she said, pointing at the two men sitting with their heads in their hands. "What the fuck happened? Why the hell are you two sitting out here just fine and my partner is back there with- well, fuck, I don't know what's wrong with her." They both stared at her, not knowing what to say. "I don't give a shit who talks first, someone tell me something that will keep me from kicking your ass and putting you back behind the doors with my partner.

The younger of the two spoke first. From his tag, she could see his name was Dillon. "She saved my life. She is back there because she saved my life." His face was badly bruised and swollen, but you could see the redness in his eyes and the tears beginning to well at the edges.

"Officer Dillon, what is your first name?"

"Mark, Lieutenant. I am so sorry. I should have protected her. It's my job, it's my responsibility."

He looked so pitiful; he actually had Sarah feeling bad for him. "You did your job by being there. She did hers and you are not the reason she is back there officer. I didn't mean to place blame on you. I am just worried. Please tell me we got the asshole that did this."

This time it was Officer Perkins who spoke. "She did. I gave chase to the brother and after apprehending him, headed back to aide Jones and Dillon. I saw Dillon unconscious on the ground and Jones was being assaulted. When I shouted out, Raul took off on foot. Jones fell to her knees, took the shot, and hit the ground. I watched Raul go down, and only prayed she saw it too before she passed out. When I got to her, she was breathing but her pulse was very faint. I called for medics and transport of the prisoners so I could ride along with her. She is one amazing woman."

Tears began to fight their way to Sarah's eyes and she felt her throat constrict as she thought about the fight Amy had given. She was so scared for her friend, but so proud of her at the same time. She managed to fight off the tears until she heard Wes' voice. He called her from down the hallway and the second she saw him, she ran into his arms and let it all go. Tears were streaming down her face and she embraced the comfort he provided. "Oh Wes, they won't tell me how bad it is, but the other officers aren't even sure how she's still alive."

Wes wiped the tears from her cheeks. "She is strong Sarah, you know she will fight and she will pull through.

Let me see if I can pull some strings and find anything out."

"Thank you. Thank you so much for being here. All these officers have shown up for support, but I didn't realize how much I needed you until I saw you." She kissed him before he turned to go find out information about Amy.

"Where is she? What happened Sarah?" Coming up behind her, Aaron looked miserable. "I was working a case when I heard. I got here as fast as I could. Is she okay? Please tell me she is okay?" He was gripping Sarah's shoulders and looked as if he might jump out of his skin at any moment.

Seeing how deeply he cared for Amy, her heart broke a little. "There is no news yet Aaron. I am sorry. Wes went back to see if he could use his weight to push for some answers."

"Good. Good. Okay, so we just sit here and wait. I don't think I can do that." He ran his fingers through his hair and paced. "Tell me something, anything."

"He is dead. I am not sure if that makes it any easier, but the shithead that put her here is dead. She got off a shot before she passed out and it went through his back into his head. He is dead," she repeated, needing to hear it one more time also.

Aaron didn't smile, but it was clear he calmed down a little with that information. He stopped pacing and took a seat in the waiting room. Sarah stayed by the doors, waiting for Wes to come back out. When she felt a hand on her shoulder, she turned quickly, hoping for news. She was more than surprised to lock eyes with Special Agent Travis Stone. His shimmering blue eyes were toned with concern and worry. He spoke very softly, "I heard what happened when I made it back to the station to set up for our meeting. I came right over. How is she?"

Frustrated and tired, Sarah relaxed under the weight of his hand on her shoulder. Sensing she needed to sit, he guided her to the chairs. "There is still no word." He sat with his hand on her back and offered support with kind words.

When Wes walked back out the doors, she jumped out of her seat. "They weren't inclined to tell me much, but I did get someone to agree to come out and speak to all of us."

"Oh my God, thank you Wes."

"I can usually put a face to most of the guys in Sarah's division," Wes said, measuring up Travis. "I don't think I have seen you around before. Are you a friend of Amy?"

Sensing a bit of tension, Sarah broke in. "Wes, this is Special Agent Travis Stone. He is here looking into some of my cases. Agent Stone, this is Wesley Porter."

"Porter? As in Richard Porter, the Mayor of New York; Any relation?" Travis asked.

"Yes, he is my father," replied Wes.

"I guess you know the right people to get the answers you need, Lieutenant. I see a doctor coming now." Travis stepped back to let Aaron move in to hear the news from the doctor, and noticed Wes lock his fingers with Sarah's. He realized Wes and Sarah were more than just friends.

"Ms. Jones made it through surgery just fine. She has a broken jaw, two broken ribs, and a collapsed lung. She is very lucky, and very strong. She is in ICU for recovery, and if she stays stable, we will move her to a regular recovery room tomorrow." The doctor saw the despair on all of their faces. "She is young and healthy. She is one hell of a fighter. She will pull through."

Sarah felt her chest tighten and wasn't sure she could speak without tears. "Can we see her?" she managed to get out.

"She is in a coma." Trying to reassure them, she continued, "It is quite normal after an ordeal like the one she went through and the extensive surgeries. It's the body's way of healing. Her vitals are excellent and she will be monitored all night. If her vitals stay the same and she remains stable, I will allow visitors tomorrow afternoon. Go home, get some rest, and I will call you if anything changes."

"I don't want to leave her here Wes."

"I will stay with her tonight," Aaron said, grabbing Sarah and giving her a huge hug. Releasing her, and realizing he didn't know her all that well, he blushed. "I'm sorry Lieutenant, I am a little out of it."

"It's okay Aaron. She is lucky to have someone care so much for her." She pulled out a piece of paper and jotted phone numbers on it. "Here is my home number, my cell, Wes' home number, and his cell. Call at any hour if anything changes." She squeezed his hand and headed toward the exit.

Travis trailed after her and Wes. "Lieutenant, may I have a word with you? It's regarding one of the cases."

She looked back at Wes and he leaned in and kissed her. "I will pull the car around front. I will drive you home tonight. You can stay at my place. Evening, Agent Stone," and he headed out for the car.

"I wanted to let you know that the brother, Jorge, rolled over. He pinned the murder of Martin James on his brother. He says the guy owed Raul money and

133

couldn't pay, so he killed him. Your girl did a good job. She closed a case and got both of those scumbags off the street. She did her job damn well."

"She is a good girl and a great cop. I don't expect any less of her. She never lets me down." Sarah felt her throat tighten again, and her mouth get dry. She wanted to escape before she got teary eyed again. She turned to leave, but he stopped her. He grabbed her hand and locked his fingers with hers. She wasn't sure why she didn't stop him.

He held her hand tight and wiped away the tear that fell down her cheek. "She won't disappoint you this time either. She is as strong as you know she is, and she will be fine." He could feel her pulse race in her wrist and hear her breath catch. He wanted nothing more than to kiss her and find out what she tasted like.

"I have to go. Wes is waiting in the car." She realized their hands were still molded together and she took hers back.

"Yes, it appears we made him wait." He brushed her hair from her face and leaned in to kiss her cheek. "Keep your head up Lieutenant, and have a good evening," he whispered in her ear then watched her walk away.

Sarah was exhausted and felt raw from too many emotions flowing through her at once. She felt herself sink into sleep before the car even made it to the first light outside the hospital. She fell quickly and silently with Wes holding her hand. She was in the conference room at the station, looking over her cases for a connection. Before she could stop it or take control of the dream, Agent Stone had her pinned against the wall. "You know you want me too," he said as he locked his lips with hers in a deep, hungry kiss. She couldn't stop herself from kissing him back. She felt this need to have her hands all over him and let him caress her everywhere. He lifted her and she wrapped her legs around his waist. He laid her down on the conference table and ripped her shirt off. She noticed Amy, Aaron, her commander, and other officers looking over files at the table, but she didn't care. They just moved as she struggled to get Travis' pants off. Why did no one care about what was happening? She wanted to stop, but she couldn't. Travis helped her get her pants off and kissed her from her neck to her feet. As he moved his tongue in between her legs, her whole body shuddered with excitement and she was jolted awake.

"Babe, are you okay?" Wes was staring at her as they pulled through the gates of his house. "You were making little noises and just about scared me to death jumping out of sleep like that."

Sarah wasn't sure what she felt. She was taken aback by the dream, but revved at the same time. "Just a bad dream. I need you, Wes. I need to feel you touch me. I feel so empty right now. I need to feel you inside me." She grabbed him and pulled him in for a passionate kiss.

"Well, unless you want me right here, let's get inside," he said as he parked the car.

Sarah was feeling so many different emotions, from grief about Amy, anger that she wasn't there to protect her, and confusion for the thoughts she was having about a man that she had just met. She needed Wes. The comfort of his touch would bring her back to reality. They entered the house through the garage and went directly into the bedroom. She walked up to him and looked him lovingly in the eyes before pressing her lips to his in a passionate kiss. She filled his mouth with her tongue as he wrapped his arms tightly around her. This was all she needed to have the stress release as she melted into his arms. He fumbled with the buttons on her shirt as he stayed engaged in their lip lock, before finally making his way to her bra. He unsnapped the clasp and released her soft breasts. His hands began to caress them, making her nipples hard. He became aware of them and began to gently roll them between his fingers, causing her to shudder. He slowly pushed her back onto the bed and removed her pants. He knelt down onto his knees and pushed her thighs apart, exposing her soft, moist area. He pressed his mouth to her and began moving his tongue rapidly in, out, and around her sex, leaving her breathless. She arched her back and moaned as he brought her closer and closer to climax when she suddenly grabbed his head and pleaded with him to stop and enter her. He stood up and removed his pants, showing off his rock hard member. He climbed on top of her and slid himself inside, causing her to moan out with excitement. He was above her, staring deeply into her eyes as he continually thrust himself in and out of her.

They kept their intense gaze as he climaxed and whispered to her, "I love you." They fell, wrapped up in each other, into a peaceful sleep.

Chapter 20

Aaron awoke at the sound of footsteps down the hallway. He had slept on a couch in the waiting area of the hospital, hoping for news. None had come, which he assumed was a good thing. That meant Amy was still stable and would be allowed visitors. A small, older woman came walking up to him.

"Are you here for Amy Jones?" she asked.

"Yes, is she alright?"

"She is awake. We will allow visitors in two hours, but you can go in and see her now," the lady beamed a smile at him when he hugged her.

"Sorry," he said, releasing her. I need to call her partner and then I would like to see her."

He followed the woman back to one of the recovery rooms. "You can have ten minutes before we need to move her. Just remember that our main concern is her internal injuries. The bruises have not been tended to and will heal on their own. She is also on a lot of pain meds at the moment. She may not be coherent."

"Thank you." He moved the curtain to the side, and instantly felt his insides shatter. Her face was almost unrecognizable. Her left eye was swollen shut with a gash above it. The entire side of her face was purple and her jaw was swollen to twice its size. He could see part of her shoulder under her gown and it was black and blue like the rest of her. She looked so fragile lying in that bed. But, he knew better than to treat her that way.

She heard him walk in and turned her head to see him. "Hey, beautiful."

"Beautiful, that's pretty freaking funny, buddy," she slurred out. "I don't even care how I look. I feel greeeeaat. You are pretty cute though. Want to hop in this bed with me? I won't tell them if you don't," she sang out.

"You must feel good," he said, grabbing her hand. "You are going to move to another room and then Sarah will get to come see you.

"Sssshhh, don't tell the boss I am high," she giggled and seamlessly fell back asleep.

Aaron went out to wait for Sarah and let out the breath he hadn't realized he was holding in. He wasn't sure how he had grown to care so much for someone he just met, but almost losing her really opened his eyes. When he found out that she was hurt, he felt emotions that he couldn't describe. The one feeling he did recognize, scared and shocked him. He was in love with her and he wasn't sure when it happened, but he was sure it was real.

Amy was sitting up in bed and happy to see Sarah walk in. Amy's face was a swollen mess, but she was smiling. Her face was almost as colorful as the flowers lining the windowsill. She was watching TV and holding Aaron's hand as he sat beside her. The bags under his eyes showed he had been there all night. Sarah was overwhelmed to see Amy awake and smiling after everything she had been through. She knew Aaron was the reason and that's all she needed to know to like the guy. "Better not get used to this lounging around shit, Detective."

"Aaron said you were coming by." Amy looked down at her lap as her eyes welled. "I am sorry,

Lieutenant. I messed up. I should have had my weapon out when the chase began."

Before Aaron could reach back over to comfort Amy, Sarah stepped in his way. "Would you mind Aaron? I would like a minute with her."

He kissed Amy on the forehead and gave her hand a gentle squeeze before walking out.

"Shut up," Sarah said, interrupting Amy. "You did great. You held your own against a man much bigger than you and still managed to give him a warning before you shot him. You went completely by the book and made me so proud. You never let up. I trained you well."

"You would make this about you, wouldn't you!" Amy laughed a little, and was forced to hold it in due to the pain. "Oh God, I still forget the extent of my injuries. As long as I don't move, it doesn't hurt."

Laughing, Sarah looked at all of the flowers. "It seems everyone else knows how great you did too. Look at all those flowers. And if I am not wrong, Aaron stayed here all night, wanting to be the first one to see you."

Amy's face lit up under the bruises and stitches. "I know. He is just so amazing. I have never felt this with anyone before." Looking down at her lap, she wondered if she should tell Sarah. "He told me he loved me this morning. He said he didn't care if it freaked me out, but he had to tell me how he felt. He loves me," she locked eyes with Sarah and began to cry.

"That's a good thing. Why the hell are you crying?" Sarah asked.

"I'm happy." Looking down at herself in the hospital bed, she laughed, "Okay, so minus the broken body and being hit by a bus feeling, I am really happy," Amy said, smiling.

"I am glad. Now get your ass better because I need my partner back." Sarah checked her phone and put it back in her pocket. "Some of us have to work. I will get Aaron and let him know the girl talk is done. I cleared three days paid time off with his Lieutenant. That's all I could get, but he is all yours for the next three days."

"Thank you, Sarah. It means a lot." Amy smiled as she watched Sarah leave the room. Life was good, she thought. She had a job she loved, a man who loved her, and a partner who was not just one of the best cops in New York, but also her best friend. She had been getting visitors and get-well messages all day. Her room was overflowing with balloons, flowers, and cards. Yes, life was pretty damn good for her, regardless of being in the hospital.

Chapter 21

It was midday when Sarah got to the station. She was getting a late start, but Amy was worth it. She knew she had to meet with Agent Stone. But, she didn't like what he did to her insides when he was around. She was even more thrown off by the dream she had about him. She blamed it on exhaustion, and a whirlwind of emotions. She tried to lock it away somewhere her brain couldn't access, but it kept sneaking back in. She was visualizing tearing his shirt off when she walked into her office. "What the f–"

"My, oh my, the mouth on you," Travis said before she could finish. "So, dirty."

Frustrated and anxious, she snapped at him. "What the hell are you doing in my office? Wait, how did you even get in my office? I lock it when I leave."

"I have my talents, Lieutenant. I would love to show you some of them sometime," he said with a wink.

Flustered, she smacked his feet off her desk. "The conference room was a fine place to meet. Get some coffee and I will bring the files in." She really needed him out of her sight for a moment.

"The coffee is already waiting for you. I take my assignments very seriously. I know your daily routine and how you like your coffee. I am sure I could guess how you like other things," he said, staring at her from head to toe.

"Get out of my office," she blurted out. "I mean, just meet me in the conference room. I need to make a personal call first."

"Fine, but I just checked on Amy. She is doing great."

Rolling her eyes at him, she sat down at her desk. What the hell was with this guy? He was getting under her skin and she was pretty sure he was doing it purposely. She just needed a minute to relax and get things back into perspective. She called Wes to gain some composure. When he answered, she was very pleased. "Hey you."

"Hey back at you, beautiful. I'm crazy busy baby, is everything okay?"

She sighed and breathed easier, just from hearing his voice. "Yeah, I just wanted to say hi and see if I was going to get to see you tonight."

"Not tonight. I pushed some serious work aside to be at the hospital last night. I have to catch up on it tonight, but I will be thinking about you. I will take you to a nice, romantic dinner when this is all wrapped up, and then you can have me all to yourself."

"Sounds good. I just need to wrap up a few things here. Then I am going to swing by the hospital on the way home and call it a night. It's been a rough couple of days."

"Yes, it has. We will have to plan a weekend getaway when things slow down. You, me, the beach, no clothes." He answered someone on the other end of the line and sounded frustrated. "I have to run babe. Stay safe and give Amy my love. I love you."

"Love you too," she said and heard him disconnect. She felt better, but she was still anxious about being in the conference room with Agent Stone. Maybe she should have let them talk in her office. She kept seeing the dream of him taking her onto the conference table. At the catch of her breath and the tingle between her thighs, she put all of those thoughts aside. She grabbed some water, and repeated a mantra of "You are a grown woman, you can do this."

Easier said than done, she thought as she walked into the conference room. There he was, with his jacket off and his white, collared shirt with the sleeves rolled up. The white shirt showed the hint of a sun-kissed tan underneath, accentuating his arm muscles. He was preparing the board with pictures and connections to each case that he had compiled. The only picture she could see was of his tight ass moving under his dress pants. Each time he moved from one corner of the board to another, she could see each cheek move with him.

Jesus Christ Sarah. He is just a man. Snap out of it.

She took a deep breath, shook her head, and walked in.

"Like what you see?" he asked her, meeting her gaze.

"Excuse me!" she stuttered out.

Staring at her for a second, he took a seat at the table. "The board. What do you think of all the information I have put together so far? There is a pretty high chance we are dealing with the same person in all of these cases.

"Oh yeah," she shook off the embarrassment and went over the board. They went over the locations and circumstances of each crime. They spent almost two hours going through the case files and making connections. She tried to stay across the table from him, but he made it a point to come sit next to her. He was close enough for her to smell his aftershave, and she couldn't dismiss how intoxicating the scent was.

She needed to get away from him, out of the room, out of the building. "It's been a long couple of days. I need to call it a day. Nice work on the board."

"Yeah, I am kind of good at what I do. That's why they gave me the Special in front of my name."

"Oh, is that why," she teased. When he flashed a smirk at her, his eyes lit up and she could feel them piercing through her. "Well, I have to go. We can finish up tomorrow," she said, standing up. She had her car keys in hand as she headed for the door, but he beat her there. He closed the door and put his back against it, blocking her retreat. "What can I do for you Agent Stone?"

Not sure of why he followed her or what he hoped to gain, he improvised, "I can pick up dinner if you can put in a couple more hours. Two heads are better than one."

"I am meeting Wes," she lied. She reached behind him for the doorknob as he leaned against the door. She looked up to meet his gaze and saw a hunger in his eyes. This was the same hunger she saw in her dream. She kept her eyes locked in his and forced herself to speak, "I have to go."

He leaned down to whisper in her ear, "We don't want to keep Wes waiting again, do we?" He moved away from the door and let his finger trail down her hand that was on the doorknob. "Have a good evening, Lieutenant."

She hurried out and got to her car as quickly as possible. She sat back with her head against the seat, feeling her body pulsing and her brain going wild. Only one word came to mind. *Shit.*

Chapter 22

Tonight, it felt good to be Lucy Lust. Sometimes the distraction of being someone else had a nice appeal. She was aware that the FBI were in town, looking into the rising body count. She was going to be on her best behavior tonight. She would enjoy the break from reality and the extra cash. She turned the radio on and found a station that put a little pep in her step as she dressed. She ate a candy bar. It was a poor substitute for dinner, but it would have to do. She savored the chocolate melting in her mouth as she twirled around the studio.

It was going to be a good night, she told herself as she walked out the door.

Four hours later, she called it a night and decided she had been right. It was a good night. She had made easy money with zero annoyances. She had three Johns who just wanted quick releases and one who just wanted to be told he was sexy and still good in bed. Her last John wanted to be spanked and told he was a bad boy. She always had fun with those men. It was rare to have a man want to be told he was arrogant and annoying. It wasn't everyday you could spank a willing man and berate and belittle him. She smiled, thinking about it as she walked back to her studio. A whole four hours had passed and she had let the rest of her world go, besides Lucy Lust. She was tired and ready for a good night's sleep. She yawned and she turned the key to her front door and shoved it open. Before she could close it shut, it slammed back open knocking her hard onto her ass.

The man slammed the door behind him and snarled at her. "I told you I would find you, you crazy bitch."

She instantly recognized the large man as the John who had tried to suffocate her with his hard-on in his car. She remembered his crazy, angry eyes reacting after she bit his erection and had him screaming. His face was distorted with rage, but he had a wicked smile on his face. Lucy stood up, backing away from him. She put her hand out in protest, "Listen, whatever you are thinking about doing, you don't have to do it. I am sorry I hurt you."

Moving across the room, he spit at her feet. "I don't want an apology bitch. I want to make you pay. And Keith is my name. You may want to remember it, because I am going to make you scream it. You are going to beg me to stop."

She backed up into the wall as he kept advancing toward her. She aimed to kick him, but he saw it coming. He caught her leg mid-air, and sent her flying across the room. She felt her whole body tremble as she landed against her vanity. Her make-up went flying everywhere and she kicked the chair over while trying to get up. She was disoriented when she stood up, but grabbed the chair and flung it at him. It hit him in the chest and had him stumbling back, but he recovered quickly. She wasn't sure she had said it, but she heard herself pleading to him, "Please stop this. You don't have to do this."

Still coming towards her, "I'm not even going to stop when you plead for mercy. I am going to show you I am a man. I'm going to show you how well my cock still works, bitch."

She pivoted and avoided him taking her out at the waist. She moved behind him and threw her arm around his throat. He clawed at her arm and gasped for air as he quickly moved backward, slamming her into the wall. Her body was being crushed between his and the wall, but she didn't release her grip. He took three steps forward and then slammed her against the wall again. The jolt of the hit had her releasing his neck and bending over for air. She sucked in a deep breath just as he grabbed her by her shirt, and shoved her down onto the futon. She kicked her legs wildly, but he used his weight by sitting on them, to keep her held down. He had both of her hands trapped in his much bigger hand. He held them at the wrists above her head.

She began to cry for help, and he slapped his other hand over her nose and mouth. "I don't think so. The only thing you get to cry for is for me. I will make you cry my name." He ripped her shirt off, rolled it in a ball, and forcefully shoved it into her mouth. She could still breathe through her nose, but the only noises coming from her mouth were small whimpers. Her brain was racing quickly, looking for an escape.

He sat above her and seemed to look right through her as he undid his belt and zipper. He yanked her pants down, ripping her panties in the process. Before she could even prepare herself, he was inside of her. He slammed his erection in and out of her with such force that her insides were trembling. He stopped, and she felt her body ease and relax a bit. He must have felt it too. "Oh, I am not done bitch. You don't get off that easy." He smiled at her and lifted her waist up. He then forcefully slid himself where she had let no man go before.

She cried out in pain. It was a kind of pain she had never experienced. Even as a prostitute, she had never felt such a violation. With each thrust she could feel the skin on her backside tearing. She hadn't realized she was crying until she felt the tear slide down her cheek.

At the sight of her tears, his face twisted with hideous excitement. He rammed himself in and out of her until he moaned like some wild animal. In his release his body relaxed and his grip on her hands loosened. She took the opportunity and used one hand to smash his nose while the other hand stabbed her fingers into his eyes. He screamed as blood gushed from his nose.

"God damn, bitch," he screamed, as they both fell to the floor. She scrambled back to the other side of the room, trying to gain some composure. He rubbed his hands across his face and looked at the blood. "Did you not have enough already? Because you sure are asking for more," he said confidently.

She caught her breath and felt his release dripping down her leg. She fought the urge to be sick and let her anger fill her instead. She took a deep breath and rushed him. She used all her body weight to lift him off his feet, then slammed her hand into his chest and shoved him down to the ground. On the way down, she heard a cracking sound. When she looked down at him and saw the blood, she realized the sound was his head crashing into the corner of the futon.

He lay there, still, on her studio floor. His eyes were glossy and blood was beginning to pool under his head. She fell to the floor, hugging her naked body. She shook and sobbed. She didn't cry for him, but for herself. She stared at him and even in death, he looked like a monster. He was now a monster she would never fear again. He was dead and she was happy about it. She took a full five minutes to cry to herself, before starting what needed to be done. She had a body to get rid of.

She calmly walked to her closet and put on clothes she was okay with throwing away. She got some towels and bandages to wrap his head. She had to avoid getting his blood anywhere else in the studio. There could be no trail left behind. When she finished covering the wound and stopping the blood flow, she rolled him onto a sheet and dragged him to the bathroom. She spent twenty minutes washing and scrubbing his body. She needed to get every piece of herself off of him. This wasn't just to erase evidence, but for her own wants as well. He didn't deserve to have any of her on him, even in death. She had kept his clothes on and let them get soaked as she washed him. When she was done, she dragged him to the window. She opened the window, looked down, and saw a dumpster three windows down.

She went downstairs, and quietly moved the dumpster beneath her window, after she confirmed no one was around. She had searched the street, and every window looking her direction. She saw no one. It was almost three in the morning and no one seemed to be stirring. The bars had closed at two, and people were already trying to sleep off their night.

Back in the apartment, she diligently cleaned the bloodstains on the floor. She used bleach and anything else she could find under the sink. She then moved the futon out to cover where he had died. She took another look at the street and surrounding windows to make sure no lights had been turned on. With the same quickness and carelessness in which he had violated her body, she tossed him out the window and into the dumpster.

She waited a full ten minutes to leave. She shoved the bloody sheet into a ball and into a trash bag. Walking to the dumpster with the trash bag, she looked around again. No one stirred. She took the opportunity and

149

moved the dumpster five windows down from hers. She threw the bag inside and walked away. She didn't care if he was found. The building had over 200 units and at least 50 that overlooked the alley where the dumpster was located. The studio wasn't in her real name, so they would have a hard time connecting anything to her.

Her whole body ached. She felt disgusting and wanted to scrub every inch of her body. She half laughed and half cried as she remembered telling herself what a good night it had been.

Chapter 23

Amy's recovery was coming along quickly, and when Sarah walked in, she learned that Amy would be released later that day. There was still quite a bit of healing needed, but she could heal with bed rest at home.

"Rise and shine lazy ass," Sarah said, walking into the room where Amy and Aaron were lip locked. "I would say, get a room, but apparently I am in it already."

Aaron's cheeks brightened with color. "Sorry Lieutenant." He turned to Amy and kissed her forehead, "I am going to go down to the cafeteria. Do you want anything?" he asked Sarah on his way out.

"No thanks, I am fine." Once Aaron was gone, she took a seat in the chair by the bed. "You can feel the love and gushiness in the air. It kind of makes me want to vomit."

Amy laughed loudly, but had to stop herself. "Damn it, Sarah. Don't make me laugh; it still hurts. He helps me go a little less crazy. But, I miss work. Fill me in."

"Agent Stone has taken over the conference room. He is going through all of our case files to see which could be connected to each other. It looks like we may have a serial killer on our hands. I wasn't sure at first, but now I have to consider it since they found Keith Simon's body in a dumpster this morning."

Amy stopped fiddling with her hair and looked up, "Isn't that the guy that came into the station freaking out about being attacked by a prostitute?" Sarah nodded in affirmation and Amy continued, "I take it he didn't put himself in the dumpster, so if you are tying it in to the other cases, then you're assuming she came back to finish the job? She didn't kill him the first time because he fought back, so she had to shut him up for good this time." Amy thought about it and put all the details together. "That's pretty damn ballsy."

"If that's the way it went down, then yes it is. It doesn't help that we have nothing, literally nothing on any of these cases. We have no evidence, and no witnesses. I don't mind asking for help when I need it. But, there is something about Agent Stone," Sarah said nervously.

"Oh yes, there is," Amy said, trying to make a sexy face. "That man is fine. He walks into a room and nasty thoughts come to mind. He just gives off this dirty thoughts vibe and you can't help yourself." Amy shifted in the bed to see out the doorway and then back into the room. "Don't tell Aaron I said that."

"I won't. I have a feeling if he knew how many men you *think* about, he may be put off." Amy smirked at Sarah's words.

"I have to get to work, but I hear you get to go home in a bit. Take the time to rest. No hanky-panky with Aaron. Promise me that, otherwise, I am going to have to have a very awkward chat with him before I leave."

"Oh, God, please don't do that. I promise," she crossed her heart with her fingers, to emphasize the point. "No hanky-panky until I am better and ready to get back to work. Keep me updated though, Lieutenant. Please," she asked as Sarah walked out and waved at her in response.

Aaron came back in the room with a coffee for himself and flowers for Amy. "More flowers Aaron! It looks like a florist shop in here already. You are crazy."

"Yes I am. I am so crazy about you." He set the flowers down and walked to her bedside. "I know we haven't known each other very long and I just told you I love you, but I want to always be by your side."

"You have been," she said while squeezing his hand. "You have been so amazing these last couple of days. I feel so blessed to have you here sleeping on an uncomfortable chair, just to be near me."

"I don't just mean here in the hospital. I want to spend my life with you Amy. I know it seems nuts to think that so quickly, but the truth is, I don't just think it. I know it." He lowered her hospital bed as far as it would go and got on one knee beside it.

At the sight of him on one knee, Amy clasped a hand over her mouth and whispered his name, "Aaron." Her eyes were beginning to swim with tears and she could feel her chest getting tight and her throat swelling.

He pulled out his handcuffs and stared lovingly into her eyes. "I know this is unconventional and I will buy you the ring you deserve, but I want to do this now." He placed one side of the cuff on his wrist and as he locked the other into place around her wrist, he asked, "Amy Rene Jones, will you do me the honor of being my wife? Will you promise to be my prisoner in love for the rest of our lives?"

She sat staring at him, tears streaming down her face. "Holy shit! Of course I will. Yes, yes, yes, I will marry you." She reached out and grabbed his shirt, bringing his lips to hers for a long, passionate kiss.

"I know it isn't how most girls see it, but I-"

"It's so perfect Aaron," she said before he could finish. "I am not most girls and it was so perfect to me. I do promise to let you handcuff me whenever you want, but get these damn things off. I have to call, well, everybody. I have to call everybody. I am so freaking happy.

Amy got so worked up that she pulled out one of her monitor cords and it sent a wild noise into the air. A nurse came rushing into the room, "Is everything okay?"

"Everything is amazing," Amy squealed out. "I am engaged."

Smiling, the nurse eyed the handcuffs. "Congratulations, but if you still want to go home today, you need to relax." The nurse hooked Amy back up to the monitor and congratulated them again on the way out.

"Oh my God," Amy said, almost flying out of the bed. "I need to tell Sarah. Get me a phone."

Sarah thought she would be hard of hearing after getting off the phone with Amy. She could practically see her smile on the other end, and had to hold the phone away from her ear to avoid the happiness blowing her eardrum out. She was pretty sure everyone in the bullpen heard, but just in case they missed it, she decided to let everyone know.

"Hey everyone, shut up," she shouted. "Detective Jones has just agreed to marry Detective Bell." She waited for the hoots and hollers of excitement to die down. "We need to put together a little welcome back and congratulations celebration when she returns. So, someone who is good at shit like that needs to get on it. I will approve, but I do not plan." She was smiling at all the excitement, and watching the officers gossip, as her eyes locked with Travis'. He was standing outside the conference room door, staring at her. He sent her a little head nod and a big smile. She felt that strange tingling in her stomach and stepped back into her office to make it go away.

He stood across the room and watched her close the office door. He had watched her before she had spotted him staring at him. Her smile was intoxicating. He had seen the happiness on her face that she felt for her friend. He wanted to walk into her office and wrap his arms around her in a warm embrace. He wanted to celebrate the good news with her and find any excuse to have his hands on her.

Sarah sat in her office doing her paperwork. She absolutely hated paperwork. She loved pulling rank and pawning it off on Amy. She really needed to recover fast and get her ass back to work. Her heart dropped into her stomach at the knock on the door. "It's open, come on in," she said, hoping it was not Travis.

"Good morning, Lieutenant." Travis shut the door behind him and sat down across from Sarah. He leaned back and propped his feet on her desk, knowing it would irritate her. He saw the glimpse of irritation cross her face and then watched her shake it off and pretend she didn't care.

"What can I do for you?" she said, looking up to catch the grin on his face. Fearing that he may voice the thoughts in his head, she cut him off, "How about we continue this in the conference room."

Travis leaned back in his chair and linked his fingers around his neck; "I quite like it in here. It's cozy."

"Are you here to help solve some murders or take a nap in my chair?" she asked, standing up. She needed to get out of this enclosed room with him. She headed to the door and swung it open. "You can't solve murders sitting in my chair. Let's go"

155

She was already out of the office and making her way to the conference room before he even got up. He figured making her wait would irritate her a little more and he loved the look on her face when she was annoyed. When he got to the conference room, he got exactly what he wanted. She was standing in front of the board with her arms crossed over her chest. She looked sexy as she tapped her foot on the floor. He walked in and took a seat. "What are the chances this was a coincidence?" he said.

"Excuse me?" she said, nervously remembering the way he had thrown her onto that same conference room table in her dream. She thought of the way his hands had felt upon her body and the way his mouth had tasted.

"Keith Simon. He makes a complaint about a hooker trying to kill him and then he ends up dead in a dumpster. Coincidence?"

"Oh." Catching her breath, she added Keith Simon's picture to the board. "He didn't seem like he was anybody's favorite person. I don't think it is a coincidence, but I am not going to rule it out. The guy was an asshole with a temper problem. He could have pissed off any number of people."

Well, if that's the criteria for getting murdered, I better watch my back," he said, grinning at her. When she rolled her eyes at him, he just laughed. "How about lunch? What are you in the mood for?"

She was frustrated with him, but she knew she was starving. "Just order a pizza or something, and let's get to work."

He ordered the pizza and they sat and reviewed the files and photos of all the cases. They sat in silence, making notes and detailing the scenes. It wasn't a busy silence, but an awkward one. So, Sarah was thrilled when the awkward silence was interrupted by the pizza delivery.

Sarah was confused why she was having such a hard time working with Travis. It was driving her crazy.

She grabbed a piece of pizza and stood in front of the murder board they had created. She turned around to say something to him and instead, she crashed right into his chest. They both looked down at his shirt, now covered in cheese and pizza sauce. "I am so sorry," she said, quickly grabbing napkins. "I thought you were still sitting down at the table."

"It's perfectly fine. It's my own fault for being so damn stealthy. It's just a hazard of the job," he grinned at her as he unbuttoned his shirt. "I keep and extra shirt in my travel bag. You just never know when you'll need one."

He removed his shirt, exposing his tanned and toned body. His chest and abs were rock hard, and she found it hard to turn away. He had a washboard stomach and perfectly toned arms to match. More and more, her dream came rushing back at her. She was waiting for him to grab her and kiss her. She was waiting for him to take her, right there in the conference room. She needed to get out of this room, and out of her head. "I need a soda," she blurted out. "Want one?"

She was almost already out the door when he answered, "Yeah, get me a regular, none of that diet shit you chicks drink."

She procrastinated with the drinks, giving him ample time to get his clean shirt on. She was relieved that his amazing body was covered when she walked back in and handed him his soda, "Here."

"Thank you," he said, sitting down again. "So, I think we should go question some of the building tenants where Mr. Simon was found."

"I usually leave canvassing to the officers," she replied.

"I just thought it might be nice to get out of here for awhile." He purposely didn't give her a chance to answer. "Great. I will drive." He was already standing up, gathering the files. "Grab the pizza, will you?"

She wasn't sure when she had agreed to leave, but decided not to argue. Maybe getting out of that room was a good idea. She grabbed the pizza and followed him out, not saying a word.

Sitting in the car next to him while smelling his cologne made her wonder if going with him was a bad idea. They were now in an even smaller, confined space together. She planned on avoiding him all together by looking out the window, but he talked the entire time. He asked her about her childhood, her interests, and her relationship with Wes. He was genuinely interested in getting to know her. He kept the conversation about her until they were two blocks from the apartment building. "I did a run on the tenants and none stick out, or have a connection to Mr. Simon. I got a couple drug busts and a domestic violence, but no one in the building screams murderer."

"Yeah, they don't really tend to." She looked up at the building, happy to be out of the car. "This is your gig pal, where do you want to start?"

"I want to start on the top floor units with windows facing the alley, and work our way down. We can get a couple of the other units too, and see if anyone heard anything." He headed up the stairs, into the building.

An hour later, they had talked to a number of people. All of them saw and heard nothing. Travis did not care. He loved watching Sarah get more and more frustrated.

"Well, this has been a complete waste of time so far," she pouted. "Some of these people actually make me feel more stupid for having spent five minutes with them."

Travis knocked on the next door and was greeted by a voluptuous blonde in a robe. She locked her eyes on Travis and came to attention. "Oh, well hello." She flashed a smile and tried to fix her hair a bit. "What can I do for you?"

The woman didn't even spare a look for Sarah. "This is Lieutenant Carmichael and I am Agent Stone. We would like to ask you some questions.

"Is this about the body they found in the dumpster? Poor man. Please come in," she said, opening her door and gesturing them in. She still never took her eyes off Travis, and almost caught Sarah's arm in the door as she closed it.

"Just let me change. Please, take a seat."

Her apartment was a small, one bedroom unit. It was bigger than the studios, but surprisingly, not much smaller than the two bedrooms. She had it decorated in what most might describe as a modern tacky look. The couch was a red and white animal print. The animal it was intended to be was unidentifiable, but it matched the living room wall that was painted the same shade of red. Sarah almost choked when she saw what the woman had changed into. She came out, prancing in a matching white tank and short set. The shorts were just long enough to show her ass and she was spilling out of the top. She had thrown a long, black lace robe on top. It obviously was not intended to cover her up, but to add flare.

The woman sat across from Travis and placed a hand on his knee. "What can I do to help?" I will assist you in *any* way I can," she said, leaning forward as one of her breasts almost escaped the tight prison it was being held in.

Trying not to act uncomfortable or annoyed at Sarah's quiet giggles, Travis just smiled at the woman. "Well, Miss-,"

"Oh, Candace Walker, but you can call me Candy," she smiled at him. "That's what my friends call me. They say I am as sweet as candy," She giggled, and her enormous breasts jiggled up and down.

Candy looked like she may cause more cavities than anything else. She looked far beyond the forty-two year old that she was. Her once brown hair was now platinum blonde with about three inches of brown roots. Her skin looked like leather from what appeared to be years of tanning, and her teeth looked as if she took her nickname too seriously.

They wrapped up the interview almost an hour later, with no information. Usually, Sarah would not have wasted so much time during an investigation. But, it was too much fun. The look on Travis' face every time Miss Candy reached over to touch his leg was priceless. She had made it very well known that she was single and looking, as she would continually lean against the sofa, arching her back to stick out her girls. Every time Travis had tried to end the interview, Sarah asked another question to keep the woman going.

Finally, they were headed towards the door. "Thank you for your time, Miss Walker," Travis said, trying not to run out the door.

"Candy," she corrected, and handed him a card showing she did private, personal massages. "If you have any other questions, well, like I said, I will assist you *any* way I can."

They walked out of her apartment and headed towards the elevator.

"You are such an asshole," he blurted out as they got into the elevator.

Sarah started laughing hysterically as the doors closed. "Oh my God, it was just too easy. How do you resist something like that?" Sarah said through her laughter.

"I have no idea," he replied, not answering her question about Candy anymore, but more about how he has resisted Sarah. He couldn't take it anymore. Watching her laugh and light up, made him react before he could sensibly stop himself. He pinned her against the elevator wall with his body and kissed her. Her lips willingly parted to his pleasure. For a brief moment, he felt her tongue entangle with his and tasted her sweet breath. Before the fuzz had cleared from his mind, she shoved him away.

"What the hell?" she said, keeping her hand out to keep him at bay. "I am with Wes. I have a boyfriend, an amazing boyfriend. You can't do that."

"That's where you are wrong. You are with someone, but I am not. I can do whatever I want," he said, stepping back towards her. "You didn't stop me at first. I know you feel what I feel."

"What I feel is that you have crossed the line."

He grabbed her hand and put it at her side with his fingers linked with hers. He stared into her eyes that were filled with lust and anger. "If there is a line, it's because you put it there. Erase it." When she sighed and closed her eyes, he leaned in again. This time, he kissed her neck and moved his hand up her stomach to her breasts. He cupped her breast as he made his way to her mouth.

Shit, she realized it wasn't a dream. She could feel his heart beating against her and the warmth stirring between her legs. She could feel his hard body leaning against hers and her head was buzzing from the taste of him. At the sound of the elevator doors opening, her mind cleared. "Fuck," she said as she shoved him away and bolted out of the building.

He caught up to her on the street. "Don't overthink this, Sarah. Get in the car and we can talk about it."

"There is nothing to talk about," she said, spinning around to face him. "That, in there, in the elevator, was a mistake; a one time mistake. I am madly in love with Wes, and will not screw that up. He deserves better than what just happened. You deserve better. You will never have me and what just happened wasn't fair to you either." She turned around and headed down the street. "I will walk. I need it."

He watched her walk away, not sure what he was feeling. Maybe it was time to take a step back. He could work on the cases from his office uptown and away from the station. He wasn't sure if he could be around her and respect her wishes, especially not now that he had felt her and tasted her. He wasn't sure he could see her again and not want to touch her or feel the way her soft lips had parted for his hungry mouth. What he did know, was he needed a cold shower, soon.

Chapter 24

Amy was so happy to be in her own bed. Wes had paid for in-home care so she could recover in her own space. She was lying in bed with Aaron, watching TV, when Wes stopped by. "Thank you again, Wes. This means a lot to me."

"Yeah, thanks man" Aaron said, rising to shake hands with Wes. "I think she will recover faster here."

"Well, you better," Wes said, kissing Amy on the cheek. "You only have the nurse for three days. I figured you would be sick of all the fuss over you by then."

"Sarah is one lucky lady. I mean not only are you a hottie, but you are a sweetheart."

"You can always make me smile, Amy. I haven't quite told her about this set up yet. She hates when I throw money around. Plus, she didn't answer her phone. Anyways, I heard you made this guy pretty lucky over here. Congratulations on the engagement. That's exciting."

"Yeah, we are pretty excited," she said, looking lovingly at Aaron. "It all just happened out of nowhere, but it just seems so perfect."

"When you know, you know. I have had a ring for Sarah for three years, but what we have is so perfect, I am not sure I want to change it or screw it up. She is so unique and what we share is truly a blessing. It has worked so well the way it is. It's the way you describe marrying him," Wes said, pointing at Aaron. "Marriage is a perfect idea to you, but how do you get better than the best. I am afraid asking her to marry me will change things."

Smiling, Amy said, "Sarah isn't like anyone I have ever met. I don't think marriage scares her, but I do know she loves simple and loves what the two of you have. If that's enough for the both of you, then there is no point in changing it. You two are great together. Plus, I get invited to all the great stuff you take her to. I love what you two have too," she giggled.

"Well, I just wanted to check in and make sure you got settled. I have to get back to work." Wes kissed Amy on the cheek, said his goodbyes, and left.

"Those two are so perfect for each other. They compliment one another so well."

Amy leaned back in bed, enjoying being pain free for the first time since the brawl. She kissed him with a hot urgency, letting him know she was ready to go.

"Amy, you know what the doctor said. You aren't ready for any physical exertion yet. You don't want to end up back in the hospital."

"I just want to play a little," she said, sliding her hand down his pants. She took him in her hand and watched his eyes light up with excitement. "It's not much of an argument, when I see how I can get you excited so quickly." She lay down on the pillow so she was flat on her back. Throwing the sheets off of her, she slid her sweatpants and panties off. "You just have to be gentle," she said, taking his hand and sliding his fingers inside her.

"I am only doing this because you are hurt and I don't want to deny you any joy." He winked at her and stood up to undress.

She loved looking at him and she still couldn't believe how fast this had all taken place. As he gently pulled himself on top of her, she looked him deep in his beautiful eyes, realizing she was about to make love to her future husband. His biceps were flexed as he held himself up and made sure to not put his weight on her.

"Are you alright?" he asked sweetly.

"Yes, I'm fine. I want you, please don't stop," she replied.

He leaned down and kissed her lips softly as he slid himself inside of her. He felt the small gasp of air escape her mouth as he gently slid himself in and out of her. She could feel the tears beginning to well up in the corner of her eyes when Aaron noticed and stopped.

"Oh my God, are you alright?" he bellowed out.

"Don't stop silly. These are tears of happiness and pleasure," she whined. "Keep going."

Aaron followed her command and continued to make love to her until she cried out from both the pleasure and pain. The climax caused her to tense her body in places that were still sore.

He brushed away the wisps of hair that had fallen into her face, and kissed her again. He then gently climbed onto his side next to her, and held her naked body until he heard her breath calm as she fell asleep. Knowing she was protected and happy, he fell into a deep sleep, holding her through the night.

Chapter 25

It's crazy how things can change in just one week. Amy had returned to work, working desk duties only, and Agent Stone had left. He left a memo with the commander, stating that he wished to work from his office until further leads came in. At this point, there were no further leads to chase, and no new murders that seemed to link to the case. There had been plenty of murders in the last week, but they had been the typical drug related type, or domestic disputes.

Sarah was relieved to not have any more run-ins with Travis. He had left the same day they had kissed in the elevator. She had spent the night avoiding Wes and stressing about how the next confrontation would go, but luckily Travis left and she didn't have to worry about it anymore. Things were slowly beginning to fall back into place. Actually, things were even better. She and Wes had spent four nights together during the week, which was very rare.

Sarah was happy. Her relationship was great, her partner was back, she closed three cases, and her main irritation had left town. For Sarah, life was great.

"I am so fucking sick of paperwork," Amy whined, falling into the chair in Sarah's office. "I mean, seriously, I am ready. Any longer, and you are going to be hunting me down because I am going to kill someone."

"A bit extreme, but okay," Sarah said, not looking up from her desk. "I have some excitement for you. Wes wants to have you and Aaron over for dinner tonight. I totally forgot to ask, kind of like you forgot to tell me that he paid and arranged for your home care. Nice slip."

Amy avoided eye contact with her. "I'm sorry. It just never came up," she lied. "Aaron has no plans, we will be there."

"You haven't even asked him. What if he has plans?"

"I am his plan. That man is the greatest. He wants to be with me all the time. I freaking love it. Well, now that I have something to look forward to, I am going to get back to work." She stopped at the door, "Tell Wes thanks for the invite."

"Uh, hello? I am the one that just invited you. Maybe you aren't ready to get back in the field, since you can't even remember who invited you and it was only a minute ago."

"You hate get-togethers. You invited me because Wes told you to," Amy laughed out loud in response to the face Sarah made. "See, I'm fine. I can still get you going," she said as she shut the door behind her.

Sarah smiled, thinking about how life was good. Actually, it was maybe a little too good. In fact, Sarah was actually a bit bored. Things were so simple and mundane at the moment. She wasn't sure if she missed the anticipation of another murder to link to this unknown prostitute, or if she missed the nervous excitement she felt around Travis. Either way, she felt a little guilty about wanting another murder to investigate, or another elevator kiss to swoon over.

She did still feel a bit of guilt about the kiss she shared with Travis, but him leaving had eased most of it. The little bit of guilt that remained had actually brought her closer to Wes. They had spent more time together and she had been more loving in the last week. He had asked a couple times what had gotten into her, but she blamed it on Amy. She said all the happiness and gooey love around the office must have seeped into her pores. Wes had shrugged it off and laughed at her description of Amy's over-the-top happiness.

Another day was drawing to an end, and Sarah was more than ready for her shift to be over. She wanted to go home, drink a glass of wine and relax. But, that was not going to happen. Wes wanted to have dinner with friends and talk about Amy and Aaron's wedding plans. He said he needed a break from work and discussing happy plans of marriage would be a nice retreat. Sarah had reluctantly agreed to the dinner, but her excitement grew when he promised to serve lobster bisque. Wes definitely knew the way to her heart.

Sarah drove straight from the station to Wes' house after her shift. She loved being greeted with a glass of wine from a handsome man. "I love the way you think," she said, grabbing the glass and giving him a soft kiss on the lips.

"And I love the way you look all the time, but you are going to change right?" Wes asked.

"Well, since you put it that way, I guess I need to." She looked down at her old blue jeans and worn out sneakers. Her blue shirt had a coffee stain on the arm from an officer's misstep earlier in the morning. "Okay, I didn't realize the day had been that cruel to me. I look like shit. I will change."

Wes cupped her chin in his hand and passionately kissed her. "Darling, it is impossible for you not to look beautiful. I just thought perhaps, clean, would be a nice touch."

"Well, you are just full of compliments today, aren't you?" She walked into the house, looping her fingers through his belt buckle. "I have time for a shower, care to join me Mr. Porter?"

The look in her eyes was wild and hungry. He knew if he joined her that a quick shower was not an option, but he couldn't resist.

She was already working his belt off with her quick hands. "You know we are going to be late if I join you for your particular brand of water games."

"I surely have no idea what you are talking about," she winked at him. "I just want my boyfriend to join me for a quick shower." She unbuttoned her shirt and threw it on the floor. "Do try and get your mind out of the gutter," she said, throwing her bra at him.

He threw her bra back at her and she turned and ran towards the bathroom. Laughter filled the house as he chased her up the stairs. He caught up to her in the bedroom where she was waiting for him. She hooked her fingers into the waistband of his pants and pulled him into her. She kissed his neck and made her way down his body as she removed his pants. She wrapped her hand around him and had him moaning with pleasure.

He unbuttoned his shirt and wiggled out of it as they kissed each other with a hunger that needed to be satisfied. "Shower," she whispered as she moved away from him and headed into the bathroom. In her wake, she left her jeans and panties on the floor.

As Wes followed her, he heard the shower turn on. They were going to be late for sure. He stood behind her in the marble shower, letting the water trickle down his back. He gently pushed her against the wall, her body facing the wall as he caressed her buttocks. He kissed her shoulders and made his way to her ear. She let out a little moan when he nipped one of them. Moving his hands down her wet body, he turned her to face him.

Her hair was wet and her eyes were bright. It amazed him that the sight of her could still take his breath away. He caressed her thigh and lifted her leg to wrap around his waist. She pulled him closer into her with that leg and they kissed each other like nothing else in the world mattered. It was just the two of them in that moment.

Wes leaned over and placed warm, sensual kisses on her breasts, licking her hard nipples with his tongue. He ran his teeth back and forth across each one slowly. Sarah tilted her head back as she ran her hands through his wet hair. He continued to tantalize her breasts with his mouth as his hands explored her wet, naked body. Making its way to her thighs, he gently slid his hand between her legs and pulled them apart. She willingly opened right up for him, accepting his fingers as they entered deep inside of her. His fingers were long, and brought her pure enjoyment as she ached for more of his touch. She closed her eyes as he moved from her breasts, down onto his knees, taking her wet throbbing area into his mouth. She let out a long sigh as she melted right into him. Sarah continued to gently stroke the top of Wes' hair as his tongue slid in and out of her. The warm water continued to course off of their skin and filled the shower with steam.

"Wes, please take me, I am so ready," Sarah pleaded as he continued to ravage her with his mouth. Wes stood up and looked Sarah in the eyes, before leaning in to absorb her mouth with a passionate kiss. He grabbed her right leg and gently held it up in the fold of his arm, as he slid his sex deep within her. He pulled out of the kiss to watch the expression on her face as he continued to thrust himself in and out of her. Sarah stared back intensely, as she felt herself getting closer to a climax. Wes enjoyed watching her while they made love, seeing her arch her body for him Sarah moaned out as she reached the end and was no longer able to take anymore. Wes followed as he watched her cry out in pleasure.

The shower had been amazing, but now all she was thinking about was lobster bisque, as the security gate buzzed throughout the house. She wasn't sure if she liked sex or food better, but she was on her way to getting both. Hence, she was a happy woman.

She buzzed the security gates open and headed downstairs with Wes behind her. She let him pick the light blue dress she was wearing. It was long and loose. It was a comfortable dress to wear around the house. It was strapless and waved along the tops of her feet as she walked, since she had chosen not to wear shoes.

They enjoyed pre-dinner drinks on the patio and Sarah was starving by the time they sat down. She didn't even care what the main course was going to be, she just wanted to dig in.

Wes passed her the bread to enjoy with her lobster bisque, and kept the conversation going. "Do you guys have a date yet for the big day?" he asked Amy and Aaron.

They looked at each other and Amy smiled brightly, "Actually, we do."

Sarah caught a glimpse of the look on Amy's face and put her spoon down. "I know that look. That look says I should be glad that I am sitting down. Amy, why do I feel like you are about to say something that is going to freak me out?"

"Well, Aaron and his mom were really close and he wants to honor her life and death by getting married on her birthday. We have discussed it in length, and I agree."

"You still didn't answer my question. Let's try another one. When is your late mother's birthday Aaron?"

Aaron looked terrified as he looked at Amy for help. "Well, it's um,"

"Oh, for Christ's sake," Amy cut in. "She is not a Lieutenant who can dress you down here. She is just Sarah, my friend," she said, staring Sarah straight in the eyes. "It's February 28th."

Almost choking on the water she had sipped, Sarah coughed and hit her chest with her hand to catch her breath. "That's one week from Saturday."

"Yes, we are well aware of when it is. And we are ready. We don't need anything big either, so we don't have huge plans to put into motion." Amy looked at Aaron and linked her fingers with his on his lap.

Wes lifted his glass. "We are very happy for you guys," he said, eyeing Sarah until she lifted her glass. "To love and a lifelong happiness," he toasted. Under the table, he ran his hand along Sarah's leg to calm and comfort her.

"I am happy for you guys." At Amy's little snort, she continued, "I am. I was just a little shocked. That's all. Don't think that my reaction means I am not happy for you."

"Well, thank you, it means a lot to us. I sort of have another shocker for you though," Amy said with a shy little smile.

"Oh God, just give me a second." Sarah downed her glass of champagne, "Okay, hit me. I am ready. What is it?"

"I would love it if you would agree to be my Maid of Honor," Amy said, smiling.

"You want me to be your Maid of Honor?"

"Well, I wasn't talking to Wes. Although he would probably look good in a dress too," she giggled out.

Amy's comment had Sarah laughing and gave her a minute to catch her breath. "Of course, Amy. You know I am not good with the girl stuff, but I will be there for you."

"Oh, perfect. Everything is just so perfect," Amy beamed.

"Well, I would like to offer my wedding gift now," Wes said as he rose and opened the curtains, showing off the large backyard. The trees were decorated with little white lights and the fountain stood beautifully in the middle. "If you haven't decided where you want to have the wedding, have it here. You can invite as many people as you want, whatever you need, just ask."

Sarah stared at Wes with her mouth wide open and her eyes as large as the moon. She closed her mouth at the happy squeals coming from Amy.

Amy tried to calm herself and stifle her excitement. "Are you sure, Wes?"

He walked over to Amy and kissed her cheek. "Of course, Amy; you aren't just Sarah's partner, you are a friend. I would be more than happy to do this for you. And you," he said, sliding his hand out towards Aaron.

Aaron accepted his hand and gave it a firm shake. "Thank you. It's nice to see her so happy."

"I am not the reason she is so happy, man," Wes said, slapping Aaron's back. "You did that to her." They watched Amy prance around in a little dance and wrap her hands around Sarah in a big hug.

Once the commotion had died down, they decided to sit down for dinner. They enjoyed lobster and cocktails while they discussed the wedding, and of course work as well. Sarah was fine discussing work, but she felt herself squirm a little every time someone brought up Travis. She didn't mind that he was gone, but she didn't want to think about the thoughts of when he had been there. She preferred to let those thoughts go.

Amy made a joke about him being so handsome that he must be gay, but Sarah knew better. Her squirm must have been more external than internal, because Wes grabbed her hand and rubbed his fingers down her back, as if to comfort her.

Dessert was crème brulee with a nice white wine. When the night came to an end, they said their goodbyes and Amy thanked Wes again, with a big kiss on the lips. "Sorry Sarah, I just had to. Now that I am getting married, I won't be able to get that in. I needed to experience it once." She looked at Aaron and gave him a kiss, "Come on, my soon-to-be hubby."

"Hey man, I would kiss you too, if it wouldn't seem weird," Aaron joked as he shook Wes' hand. "Thanks again."

They walked in the house, hand in hand, and Wes spun her around to dance with her right in the foyer. "You seemed a little off tonight. Is something bothering you?" Wes asked.

"No," she blurted out. "I guess I am just a little thrown off with how fast everything is moving. It was just last month that they met each other."

"Sometimes that is just how it works. You can't judge them. Everyone is different." He spun her around and danced them into the parlor. "That wasn't what I was talking about though. Every time Amy said anything about Agent Stone, Travis, you seemed uncomfortable."

Sarah stopped dancing and made her way to the mini bar. She poured herself a glass of wine. "I just wasn't his biggest fan. He came in and tried to take over my investigation. You know how much I hate that."

He came up behind her and set her glass down. He rubbed his hands down her arms and turned her to face him. "It seemed like more than a slight irritation. Was there something going on between the two of you?"

She shoved his hand away and stormed away from him to the couch. "Are you serious? You must be out of your mind. I thought you and I had something deeper than that. How can you ask me that?" Sarah could feel her heart pounding against her chest. She was trying to let her anger overwhelm her guilt. She didn't want to tell him in fear of hurting him. It wasn't her fault. He kissed her. She didn't do anything wrong, she told herself.

But, she had. She had let him kiss her and she thought about it every day since. She knew that was wrong.

Wes met her at the couch and sat down while she paced. "Sarah, you still haven't answered my question. You can be as mad at me as you want, but you still haven't answered the question. Was something going on between you and Agent Stone?" Wes asked again.

She stopped pacing and realized the anger only made the guilt worse; it made her look guilty of something, and she wasn't, she reassured herself. She sat down on his lap and cupped his face with both hands. "Of course not. I love you Wes, only you. There will never be anyone else." She kissed him deeply and let him feel the passion that was flowing through her.

"That's all I needed to hear," he whispered into her ear as he laid her on her back and moved above her.

His hand slid under her dress and up her thigh. He made his way slowly to her panties, enjoying every shudder her body let out for him. He gently removed her panties, tossing them to the floor, and entered her hungrily awaiting body. He loved the softness and femininity of the dress and wanted her to leave it on. He used his skilled fingers to undo a few of the buttons, exposing her soft breasts; they were being held in by a powder blue, lace bra, which just slightly hid her perfectly pink nipples. Wes pulled the bra down, leaving her hard nipple exposed.

As he continued to move in and out of her, his mouth made his way to her nipple and he gently nibbled it, sending waves of electricity through her body. She begged for more, as he slid her other breast out and gave it the same pleasurable treatment.

He always knew how to get her blood coursing through her body. He could feel the heat escaping from her entire body. She moaned and arched her back with pleasure. He looked up at her and she turned her head to the side, exposing her bare neck. Knowing how much she loved her neck nibbled, he accepted the silent invite and gently kissed and bit her neck. It wasn't just a nibble. It had a sting to it that made Sarah's body quiver and tingle all over. He could feel her body tighten around him as he made his way to her ear and began to slightly wet it with his tongue. He blew softly, leaving tiny little goose bumps all over her body. He did this until they both climaxed together.

Wes had an early morning meeting, and Sarah had the day off from work the next day. So, she decided to go home for the night. She kissed him goodnight and relished at the thought of being able to sleep in.

Chapter 26

A sense of dread crept into Lucy's belly as she inserted her key into the door to her studio. She hadn't returned since she had killed a man in her living room. It wasn't just the death that bothered her, but the memories of the torture he had put her through. It wasn't guilt that made her sick to her stomach when she walked in. It was pain that ripped through her body as she thought about how he had defiled her in that very room.

She looked around and was pleased that there was no sign of what happened. The cleanup was thorough and time consuming, but she was certain there were no signs of murder. This was a secret and a burden she would bear on her own. Lucy hadn't worked in over one week, and the flashbacks of that night made her think she might need to wait longer. She did not want to be in that room. She couldn't bear to look at her couch and think about him on top of her, forcing himself inside of her.

She cringed and crossed to the other side of the room to be as far away from the couch as possible. She felt better sitting at her vanity, unable to see the memories in the mirror. Slowly, but surely, her mood lifted and she shut out the thoughts that would distract her from work. She needed money, and just felt like she needed to be Lucy again for a night. She needed to escape her reality and let go in a way she could only do when she was Lucy. She knew the cops were at a dead end with the recent murders and felt very safe to go out tonight. She was confident that she couldn't be tied to any of the dead bodies. She had worked very hard to make sure of that.

The headache that had been creeping up the base of her skull began to retreat as she applied her make-up. She lightly bronzed her skin and applied emerald green eye shadow. The shadow sparkled in the light as she turned to choose a wig. She chose one of her favorites. It was the long, fiery red one with wavy curls that would end just above her butt. She chose piercingly green contacts to finish off the look. She smiled at herself in the mirror and loved being able to be someone else, when she wanted.

Sometimes you just need an escape, and to be someone else, she thought.

But, she wasn't just anyone else. She was Lucy Lust.

She felt Lucy needed to be sexy, as she made her way to her closet. The weather had warmed up a bit, but not enough for the dress she was considering. She wanted to make money, but not freeze her ass off at the same time. She continued looking for something eye-catching, but comfortable too. She stopped when she saw one of her favorite dresses. It was a short, black dress with long sleeves. The length would show off her legs, but the sleeves would keep her warm. She put on a black lace thong and matching bra. She slid the under dress on before gently sliding the lace over her body. The dress clung tightly to her body, accentuating her perfect female figure. The curves of her breasts, the lines of her hips, and the flatness of her stomach were displayed perfectly.

Her four-inch high, black lace heels matched perfectly with her dress. She slid them on her feet and took a final look in the mirror. She felt pretty good, until she turned around and found herself staring at the couch. She was assaulted by images of that night, and pain tore through her body again. She fought back the bile rising in her throat and had to sit down at her vanity.

Breathing in and out several times, she calmed herself down. She waited for her throat to open again, and her muscles to relax. Her whole body was stiff as she fought to regain control. The fuzziness in her brain was beginning to dull as she continued to breathe steadier with each second that passed. Once she calmed, she headed out the door, making sure to avoid looking at anything but the door as she walked out. She needed to get out of the room, and she planned to stay out of it for quite awhile, for work.

It was only 11:30pm when she came out of her apartment, but she figured the early start gave her extra time to make money. She knew the bars were not closing down until later, so she headed towards one of them that she knew offered privacy booths. She also knew, from experience, that regardless of the time of night, men often thought about sex. She knew there was money to be made.

The club was on a corner that was lit up with various colors of lights, and flashing signs of alcohol logos. When she walked up, a man was already being thrown onto his ass. Apparently, it wasn't too early in the night, after all. The place was crowded and there was a line to get in. She stood far enough for the men in line to get a glimpse of her. She noticed quite a few of them eyeing her, and several of them were getting dirty looks from the women they were with.

Lucy laughed to herself when one of the women was irritated by her presence, enough to shout out that she was a whore. That single word urged everyone in line, as well as some in the club, to look in her direction. Lucy kept her backside towards all of them, and she did not let the insult offend her. This could actually be good for business. Now, she didn't need to make it known that she was working. In addition, now no one would be afraid to ask for what they needed.

The club proved to be a great idea. Three hours had passed and she had serviced four Johns. Only one of them had wanted the full package. The other three just wanted a quick oral fix. She obliged to their needs, collected her money, and moved on.

She was pleased with the night's events, as she left the club. It was a nice evening, one that offered her no stress. She didn't feel guilt, and the men were all as gentlemanlike as they were capable of. It was exactly the type of night she needed on her first night back to work. It was a great way to get back into the flow of things.

As she walked down the street, back towards her studio, she heard shouting. She peeked around the corner and saw a young couple arguing. They were maybe about twenty years old, and the girl was sobbing. The boy, who appeared to be her boyfriend, was shouting at her and calling her names. He was accusing her of cheating on him, while screaming obscenities at her. She denied everything he said, and cried each time he called her an insulting name. She begged him to stop yelling at her, but her tears only made him yell louder.

When the young girl tried to reach out and hug him, he grabbed her arms in protest and pushed her back against the wall. As her sobbing became wailing, he screamed at her more, telling her to shut up.

When she realized it was none of her business, Lucy continued down the street. She couldn't risk another altercation, and having to be part of a police report. She turned to walk across the street.

She suddenly heard a loud noise, followed by begging and pleading. "Please stop. You're hurting me. No," was the last thing she heard the girl scream out. Lucy walked back to the street and at the same second, the young man hit the girl in the face and sent her skidding onto the ground. When she tried to get up, he kicked her in the ribs and she doubled over, crying. The young girl tried to say something to him, but before she could get the words out, he kicked her again. This time, his foot met her face and her body fell limply to the ground.

He stood over her body, raking his fingers through his hair. When he noticed Lucy watching, his face turned stark white and his eyes were as big as the moon. A little bit of fear, panic, and anger all swept across his face.

The anger overruled the others. "What the fuck are you looking at?"

Lucy ignored him and kneeled over the girl. Her face was covered with blood and her body had signs of bruising from previous fights. She felt a great deal of relief when she felt the girl still had a pulse.

"Get the fuck away from her," he shouted as he approached Lucy.

"I am checking for a pulse and making sure she is okay. I am pretty sure you would rather get charged with assault and not murder, so why don't we get her to a hospital."

"Charged? I am not getting charged with anything. Nothing happened. No one is going to believe what a whore says."

"It's obvious that you don't care about this girl so just go home. I will take care of her and make sure she gets the help she needs. I will make sure you never see her again."

"Like hell you will!" he said, springing forward and leaping at Lucy.

Lucy expected him to do something stupid out of anger, and was positioned perfectly to pivot out of his way. He stumbled, lost his footing, and ended up face first in a pile of trash bags. He rolled over and his face was flushed red with rage. He was breathing heavily and trying to get up.

"Let it go kid," Lucy said, getting ready for him to come at her again. "It's not worth it. Just call it night and go home."

"Who the fuck are you, to tell me what to do?" he screamed as he came flying at her again.

She used his momentum to drive him into the ground as she caught him in the chest and took him down. "I am the woman who is going to show you that not all of us will sit and take a beating. If you don't leave, I am going to be the woman who ends up kicking your ass." She held him to the ground with her hand around his throat and her knee at his groin.

His breathing steadied and she could feel the pulse in his jugular begin to slow. "Fine" he said, as he laid his hands at his side in defeat, "Let me up."

"I'm not stupid, kid. I have given you a pretty good offer. Take it." She moved her knee away from his groin and waited to see if he would try to lunge again. When he didn't, she released her hand from around his throat and stood up above him. "Don't do anything stupid when you get up. Otherwise, I will kick your ass and then have you charged with her assault," Lucy said as she pointed at the young woman lying unconscious on the pavement. "She deserves better than this. She deserves better than you."

He slowly stood up and stared at Lucy. When she didn't say anything, he turned and started to walk away. She turned and went back to the girl. She was kneeling over her, checking her vitals, when she heard footsteps behind her. She heard them just in time to avoid the full kick to her back, but she still got hit in the side, enough to make her lose her balance. She scrambled back away from him quick enough to avoid another kick and be face to face with him.

"God damn it kid. I told you to let it go."

"Fuck you," he shouted as he came at her again. His anger had him swinging blindly and off balance.

Lucy pushed him into the wall and when he turned at her again, she kneed him in the groin, turned, and elbowed him in the face. He fell to the ground and didn't get up. He was knocked out and lying next to the young girl he had done the same to.

Lucy stood, staring, not sure what to do. She didn't know if she could kill such a young kid, but she couldn't risk him exposing her. If she killed him and left him where he was, there would be another police investigation. Could she really risk that when she was so close to a club known for prostitution? Could she really risk the cops putting the facts together? The kid had just beaten his girlfriend. What were the chances he would go to the cops with a story about a woman beating him up? Lucy knew she ran a risk no matter what. So, she left the alley and found a pay phone.

"911, what's your emergency?"

"I just saw a guy robbing and attacking a young couple. I think he was on drugs." She gave the dispatcher the location, hung up before she could be asked any questions, wiped the phone clean, and walked away. Hopefully that could keep her in the clear for now. If the kid is smart he won't say anything. Lucy was hoping she didn't have another problem on her hands.

I am not a killer. She kept repeating the words in her head, as she walked to the studio. *I have only hurt those I had to protect myself from. It's not my fault there are so many assholes out there.*

She had let the kid go even though he had hurt an innocent young woman and then tried to attack her too. Lucy protected herself, but what about protecting that girl? By letting him go, he may never learn from his mistakes.

She couldn't worry about that now. As she heard the sirens in the distance, she walked down the street pressed tight against the buildings, to avoid the illumination from the street lamps. She pulled her hair in front of her face and walked quickly with her head down. She wondered why life had taken such a crazy turn. She had been playing Lucy for so long, with no problems. But, ever since that one night at the Millennium Hotel, her life had changed drastically. It seemed as though she couldn't go one night now without a confrontation. It made her sick to her stomach, wondering if subconsciously she enjoyed it and went looking for it.

She shook those thoughts clear out of her mind as she approached her building. Of course she didn't go looking for trouble. She just wanted to make her extra money each night, and go home. None of this was her fault.

None of this is my fault. She said the words like a mantra, until she was inside. She just wanted to lie down

185

and get off her feet. As she remembered she only had the couch in the studio, she let out a little whimper. She was pretty sure she would never be able to use that couch again. She would find the time to get a new one, but for now, she needed to change and get home, her real home, and her real bed. Her reality.

Chapter 27

"How am I supposed to plan a wedding on my days off when we get called in on our days off?" Amy whined in the elevator on the way up to the bullpen.

She was in tight blue jeans and a black sweatshirt that looked two sizes too big. It was obviously Aaron's. Her hair was pulled into a messy ponytail and she hadn't fussed much with her make-up. She took her days off very seriously.

"First off, when the commander says come in, we come in. Second, most people give themselves more than one week to plan a wedding," Sarah pointed out. "I know, I get it. I am not giving you shit," she cut in before Amy could whine some more. "I was just pointing out the facts. Please tell me you brought clothes just in case we have to go out in the field, or heaven forbid, meet with the commander."

Amy rolled her eyes. "Of course I did. I just left in a hurry and didn't want to change." Looking around the bullpen, she was happy to not see the commander. "What's up anyway?"

"A new possible lead in the prostitution killings we were working on," said a much too familiar voice.

"Oh, fuck me sideways," was Sarah's response when she turned around and was face-to-face with Travis Stone.

"Well, that's a nice welcome back. Hello, Lieutenant," he said, smiling at Sarah. "Detective," he said to greet Amy, while keeping his eyes locked on Sarah.

Feeling the tension, Amy butted in, "I am grabbing the Lieutenant her coffee. Would you like some, Agent Stone?"

"I would love some. Thank you, Amy." This time he met her gaze and smiled at her as she turned to get coffee.

Sarah didn't miss the opportunity to move around him and headed to her office. She prayed he was not following her, but she could hear his footsteps behind her. She also heard him stop the door from closing, which she tried to shut before he could enter her office. "What are you doing back here? I haven't gotten any word on any new murders or leads."

"Yes Lieutenant, it's nice to see you too." He sat down with his feet on her desk, knowing it would bug her. "Now that the pleasantries are out of the way, we can get to work. Dispatch got an anonymous call last night, saying a young couple was being robbed and attacked by a man. The caller thought the attacker might be on drugs. When officers arrived, there was a young woman unconscious and a young man who had obviously been assaulted. Officers asked him where the man was who attacked them and he screamed at them, claiming the attacker was a whore. His exact words were," he had to look at his notes to confirm. "It was a crazy hooker bitch. She came out of nowhere and started hitting my girlfriend and demanding money. That's the girl I love so I was like in there right away, on top of her. She was huge and so strong. She just whaled on me and then I don't remember anything else." He put his book away when he finished reading the statement.

Sarah took a minute to process what she heard. "So this kid says he and his girlfriend were attacked by a prostitute who left them unconscious and tried to take their money? How does that connect to our killings? They are still alive."

"Hey, the kid said it was a crazy hooker. Those two words got my boss jumpy and he sent me back down here to investigate. She left Keith Simon alive, for a little while at least. Plus, there was no robbery. Both of them still had their wallets."

"So, wouldn't you think she would learn from her mistake after leaving Keith Simon alive, even momentary as it was? Why leave these kids alive if it's the same girl? She likes to cover her tracks. I don't get it. What did the girlfriend say?"

"The girl is in a coma." He saw Sarah's face tighten a bit. "Yeah, this one is a little different. She has never gone after a couple or a woman before. I'm not sure how the pieces connect, but that's why I am here. There will be a briefing in the conference room in," he looked down at his watch, "fifteen minutes."

"I will get my files together." Hoping he would get up and leave her office, she went back to work. When she noticed he hadn't gotten up, she met his gaze. "Was there something else Agent Stone?"

"No. I was just enjoying a few moments of down time," he replied, enjoying the way she squirmed in her chair.

Uncomfortable in the small, confined space with him, she stood up and gathered her paperwork. "I have what I need, see you in the conference room," she said as she headed towards the door, avoiding eye contact with him.

He cut her off before she could get to the door and blocked it with his body. It happened so quickly that she almost slammed into him. "Get out of my way. I have work to do," she demanded.

He stood there for a moment, taking in her scent and feeling the tension emulating out of her. "I have missed your politeness. Let me help," he said, reaching for her files. He purposely ran his fingers along her wrist as he grabbed some of the files from her.

"Thank you." Seizing the opportunity with his hands partially full, she opened the door right into him and stepped out. She could hear him laughing behind her. It was a laugh that told her he knew he had gotten to her. She cursed herself for letting him see it.

"Lieutenant, are you okay?" Amy asked, coming up beside her.

Jumping back, Sarah said, "Jesus Amy, you startled me." She raked her fingers through her hair and rubbed her eyes with the balls of her palm. "I am fine. Take these files to the conference room. I will meet you there."

Sarah went to the bathroom and splashed cold water on her face. She just kept telling herself to get a grip. But she wasn't the one doing anything. It was that damn man. He tried to get her going every chance he got, and he found the chance quite often. Things were so much easier when he had left. She needed to prove that this new assault case could not be linked to the killings so he could leave again.

As she walked into the conference room, she saw Amy and Travis gabbing like schoolgirls. Travis had just said, "I would love to," as she walked up behind them.

Not caring if she was rude, Sarah cut right in, "Would love to what, Agent Stone?"

His eyes lit up as he smiled and devilishly replied, "Well, Amy here was just letting me know that if I was in town this weekend that I was invited to her wedding. Wasn't that sweet of her, Lieutenant?"

"Oh, just the sweetest." Sarah had to grit her teeth to keep her from strangling Amy.

"I do believe she said it was at Wesley Porter's place. Is that right?"

"Yes. Wes offered his place as a gift. He is not just my boyfriend, but also a good friend of Amy's, and an all around amazing man." It was quick, but there was a quick flash of irritation over his cool exterior.

"He sounds just extraordinary. Amy is lucky to have such a great friend." Travis turned to head to the board, a little annoyed. He grabbed Sarah's arm as he turned and whispered in her ear. "I was talking about you Lieutenant. Amy is lucky to have you as a friend. If I can't have what I want from you, then I will make you my friend at least."

He released her arm and ran his fingers along hers. They were behind everyone, so no one could see, but she had to steady her body and face to make sure her reaction would not bring alarm to anyone. She felt like crawling out of her skin and wanted to run out of the room. "We will see," she said as she walked to the board. She had a job to do and she wouldn't let him get in the way of it.

After the briefing, Travis caught up with Sarah in the hall. "So, I have an interview with this kid from last night. Travis Decker is his name. Nice name, right?" he winked at Sarah. "Anyway, you want in on the interview?"

"When you have more concrete information maybe. But, I don't think it is a good use of my time right now. He's all yours pal." Sarah turned and headed back to her office.

"Save me a dance this weekend, Lieutenant," he said as he walked away. He said it just loud enough for a few cops to look her way. She turned around and gave him an icy glare that had him laughing as he walked back to the conference room.

Sarah sat at her desk with her head in her hands. She was fighting off the stabbing pains crawling up the back of her neck, when there was a knock on her office door. "Oh, for the love of God, can I get five minutes without you pestering me?"

"Actually, no," Amy said as she walked in. "As Maid of Honor, that is not a luxury you get."

"I'm sorry, I thought you were Agent Stone coming in to bug me about something irrelevant again."

"Yeah, what's up with that? I think I would literally melt into a pile of goo if he looked at me the way he looks at you. What's up there?" Amy asked, leaning her elbows on the desk as she waited for some juicy gossip.

"Not to disappoint you, but nothing. For some reason, the man finds it entertaining to irritate me." Almost to feel reassured, she said it again, "There is absolutely nothing going on."

"Maybe not on your part, but he looks at you like he is a fat kid and you are a big, sweet piece of sugary cake."

"I don't have a comment for that. I am not even sure where you get half the stuff that comes out of your mouth," Sarah said, disparagingly.

Amy leaned back in the chair and flashed a huge grin at Sarah. "Speaking of cake, will you come with me tonight to pick a flavor? Aaron has to work and he said it's cool if I pick it. Plus, you can help me pick my dress while we are out. I have a couple picked out, but I want your opinion. We also need to pick out a dress for you."

Sarah was not a fan of weddings or shopping, but she had agreed to be the Maid of Honor, and Amy's smile meant that saying no was not an option. "Sure, I would be happy too." Feeling obligated but nervous, Sarah sucked it up and spit it out, "Is there anything else you need me to do?" She was hoping the answer was no.

"Actually, you dating the best guy in the world is enough. He already had a planner contact me, and we have done everything else over the computer. It's been so easy. She sends us pictures and stuff and Aaron and I pick out what we want. We have already picked the color scheme, the band, and the food. Wes has helped us out so much by letting everything happen out of his house. He has also helped coordinate the deliveries around his schedule, so he can do spot checks and make sure everything is perfect. He really is great," she dreamily sighed out.

Travis walked by Sarah's office, sending her a naughty grin as he passed. "Yes he is," Sarah agreed with Amy.

Sarah had managed to stay in her office for most of the day, and let Travis handle the infield work. She didn't normally delegate her work, but it was technically her day off and she wanted nothing more than to avoid Travis completely. The thought of getting trapped in a room or elevator with him again, had her heart racing. Luckily, when she had wrapped things up for the day, Amy popped in her office, ready to go. At least now, if Travis ended up in the elevator, she wouldn't be alone. She was actually looking forward to dress shopping, over seeing Travis again. Sarah didn't care what the excuse was, but she wanted to get out of the building.

It was not only her duty as a friend, but also as the Maid of Honor, to sit in the waiting area of the dress shop, in pure boredom. Sarah sat on a plush, white sofa and waited for Amy to come out in each dress. She patiently sat, waiting to ooh and ahh each dress. She was thankful the shop provided complimentary champagne. It helped ease the headache she had coming on. Amy had tried on five dresses already, and Sarah didn't see much of a difference between any of them. They were long and white, and looked like wedding dresses. The whole ordeal baffled her, which was probably why she wasn't married yet.

Amy appeared from behind the curtain in another dress. This one was long with a plunging back. She twirled as she admired herself in the mirror. "Maybe we shouldn't have done the cake testing before the shopping. I feel like a cow."

"You have looked great in every dress you have tried on," Sarah said, sipping her champagne.

"I know you hate this, but I just can't decide," Amy pouted.

"I honestly don't see much difference in any of them, but if I had to pick, I like the second one you put on.

"Oh, me too," Amy exclaimed with excitement. "That was my favorite too. Sweet, I have my dress." She turned to the sales associate and jumped up and down. "Number two it is. Please wrap it up and we will take it to go," she giggled out. "Now it's time to pick your dress, and then I promise you can go home."

"Oh, goody," Sarah said quietly to herself as Amy headed back into the fitting room to change.

Two hours later, and with a massive headache, they had agreed on a Maid of Honor dress. Amy had made Sarah try on what seemed like a hundred dresses. In reality, it was probably closer to a dozen, but Sarah was exhausted. There were a couple of times throughout the evening that she was glad she had left her weapon in her vehicle. There were several moments throughout the evening that Sarah fantasized about hurting the saleswoman.

The woman, who was named Maggie, was tall, thin, and blonde, with a voice high enough to shatter glass. She squealed over every dress and fussed with it before Sarah could exit the dressing room.

Amy had realized Sarah's annoyance, and found the dress she loved on Sarah, just in time. Amy noticed Sarah was going to burst, and wanted to make sure she knew she appreciated her effort. "Thank you again, for spending the evening with me. I am glad we found something we both love," Amy said, smiling.

"Uh huh," Sarah replied.

"Well, that's it. Everything is done. I am ready to get married," Amy said gleefully. Her smile lit up her whole face.

"I really am glad that you are so happy, but I am calling it a night." Sarah gave Amy a hug and congratulated her again on her way to the car. It was time to go home and put her feet up, with a nice big glass of wine.

Chapter 28

Lucy Lust was scratching at the surface, begging to come out. But, there was no way she could come out to play tonight. Too much had happened when she was allowed out. She saw on the news that the young man from the night before had gone to the police. The sniveling little weasel had actually told everyone that he and his girlfriend were attacked and robbed by a crazy prostitute.

He described her as big as a house with monster-like eyes. He said she was raging out of control from drugs and that was the reason he was beaten up by a woman. He claimed he was attacked while trying to protect his girlfriend who was now in a coma.

"Bullshit," Lucy screamed when she was let to the surface for a moment.

How could that little twit not remember repeatedly kicking his girlfriend when she was already down? And, as big as a house? That kid was so ashamed of getting beat up by a girl, that his lies brought the case further away from the truth.

Of course, the media was trying to connect the dots between the cases, but the police and FBI confirmed that at the current time, there was no concrete connection between murders.

The stunningly handsome face of Special Agent Travis Stone was on screen, and he announced that they were looking for any new leads that would connect the new case to the serial murders he was investigating. He assured the public that they would be the first to know if a connection could be made, then gracefully turned down any further questions and walked away.

Lucy was a little excited to have the FBI after her. She knew it was wrong, but she felt a rush when she saw the broadcast. It was the first time the FBI had confirmed they were involved in the investigation. She also wondered what it would be like to let Agent Stone catch her. She imagined his hard body holding her down and handcuffing her. The image had her tingling between her legs.

The newswoman's face flashed on screen and she had a warning for her viewers. "Be cautious of who is around you at night, and if you have any leads about this vicious murderer, please come forward. The station is working on putting together a reward to help get this monster off our streets."

"Vicious murderer, my ass," Lucy screamed as she threw the remote at the television. "Why isn't anyone reporting about who those men were? What nasty pigs they were? Cheating husbands, rapists, and woman abusers are getting sympathy on the evening news. Pfft, what is our world coming to?" she wondered as she headed off to bed. It was time to put Lucy and herself to bed for the night.

Chapter 29

Time had passed quickly, and her big day was here. Amy stood in her bridal tent in Wes' expensive backyard. He had made sure she had the works. A personal hair stylist and make-up artist had been provided for her, at his request. The tent came with a small mini bar and a cozy, plush white couch, which Sarah was relaxing on.

"It's a freaking circus out front," Sarah said, fussing with the curls of her up-do. "One of the vendors must have spilled the beans about wedding plans here and the whole city thinks Wes Porter is getting married. It cracks me up. I bet his mother is having a hissy fit."

"Yeah, Aaron sent me a picture from upstairs, of all the news vans outside. Wow, are they going to be let down when they find out it's just little old me," Amy smirked.

"Well, little old you, looks beautiful," Sarah beamed as she snapped a photo with her phone. "In less than one hour, you will be Mrs. Bell. Are you excited?"

"I'm extremely excited, with a mix of nausea," she giggled while rubbing her belly to calm it down. The dress she had chosen was a white lace gown with a three-foot long train. The waist was covered in embroidered crystals. The sleeves were completely lace that stopped just above the wrist. The dress barely sat on her shoulders, leaving her back exposed. The plunging backline stopped at only three inches above her buttocks.

It was sexy, but in an extremely classy way. She had the perfect body for the dress she picked.

Sarah stood up and walked to stand in front of the mirror with her. The dress they agreed on for her was a spaghetti strap, sky blue dress. It flowed back and forth as she walked, and it was just long enough to leave a peek of her matching heels at the bottom. It was simple, yet elegant, and it matched the wedding color theme perfectly.

Amy and Aaron had agreed on a beautiful blue and white color theme. The color scheme worked out, so it looked like a blue sky with white clouds. From the tents, to the cake, to the chairs, everything matched the theme perfectly.

Sarah draped her arm around Amy before giving her a supportive pat on the behind. "You ready kid? It's about that time."

"Give me a glass of champagne, and I will be ready," she said, taking Sarah's glass and downing it. "Hell yes, I am ready."

In the groom's tent across the lawn, Aaron finished off his tuxedo with a sky blue bow tie and waistcoat. He could feel his nerves biting away at his stomach.

"You look like you could use a drink," Wes said as he entered the tent. He poured a small shot of brandy into a glass and handed it to Aaron.

"Thanks, man. I'm not having cold feed, I'm just nervous as hell," he said, sipping the brandy.

"I would say there was something wrong with you if you weren't nervous." Wes poured himself some brandy and adjusted his bow tie in the mirror.

"Thanks again, for everything. This turned out beautiful. I am not sure how you pulled this off on such short notice."

"It's a little thing I call, being the Mayor's son. It has its perks. People like to jump when you ask for something." He clinked glasses with Aaron in a toast. "I'm glad your dad could make it down on such short notice."

"I am glad to. Most of my friends moved out of state and couldn't make it on short notice, but I don't care about that. Amy is the only one I need out there with me." Aaron sat on the couch and sipped his Brandy. "I am appreciative you stepped in to be best man. It works out well; Amy and I, and you and Sarah up there. You both did so much to make today possible, even though I know the Lieutenant doesn't approve."

Wes patted Aaron on the back, "She doesn't disapprove. She just has different views on things. Marriage isn't even a blip on her radar. She approved of you, and making Amy happy. That's all that matters. It's time. Are you ready?"

Aaron finished his brandy and stood up. He took one last look in the mirror, and headed for the altar. "Hell yes, I am ready," he said emphatically.

Sarah wished Amy luck and took her place at the end of the aisle to begin her walk. She held a bouquet of blue flowers and knew her officers were going to give her shit for the dress and flowers. The blue and white chairs were lined with blue lilies and filled with officers in their dress blues. It was an amazing sight.

Instead of a long red carpet leading to the altar, there was a long blue and white aisle. Sarah kept her eyes on Wes, who was standing at the altar with Aaron. It was easier than acknowledging the looks from the cops who were used to seeing her in jeans. She made her way to the end of the aisle, took her position, and looked back towards where she knew Amy would appear.

At the sound of the wedding march, Amy appeared and linked arms with her father. She had a huge smile on her face as she made her way to Aaron.

As Sarah looked to Amy and watched her, she caught Travis gazing from the crowd. She felt her stomach clench as soon as they locked eyes. She forgot that Amy invited him. He kept his eyes locked on Sarah and sent her a wicked smile. In response, she looked away and caught Wes' stare. For a moment, she thought she saw a flash of anger on his face. But, it was wiped away quickly by a smile, and he blew her a kiss.

Amy handed her bouquet to Sarah and linked hands with Aaron. He smiled at her and began his vows:

"I Aaron, take you Amy, to be my wife, partner in life, and my one true love.

I will cherish our union and love you more each day, than I did the last.

I will trust you and respect you, laugh with you and cry with you,

Loving you faithfully through good times and bad,

Regardless of the obstacles we may face together.

I give you my hand, my heart, and my love, from this day forward,

For as long as we both shall live."

When he finished, Amy had a tear streaming down her face but choked her emotions back and said her vows.

Instead of exchanging rings, Aaron and Amy each locked one side of a handcuff to the other's wrist. Their giggling made everyone laugh.

The ceremony ended with the words, "I now pronounce you husband and wife. You may now kiss the bride." Everyone applauded as Aaron and Amy shared a very long, passionate kiss, then raised their cuffed hands in the air. They walked to the end of the aisle hand in hand then undid the cuffs. Aaron picked her up in his arms and swung her around, kissing her again, before putting her back down. Everyone was clapping and shaking their hands as they made their way to the reception.

Wes arranged a large white tent lined with blue lights to serve as the reception area. There was a large head table, set for seven. The bride and her parents, the groom and his father, and Sarah and Wes would sit at the head table. All of the guests took their seats and a four-course meal was served. Amy and Aaron chose an appetizer of calamari, followed by a fresh Caesar salad, and lobster bisque. The lobster bisque, of course, was chosen in honor of Sarah. The main meal was lobster tail and filet mignon. The meal was superb, and the ambiance was beautiful. There were absolutely no complaints.

"You overdid yourself Wes," Amy said, kissing him on the cheek before she and Aaron moved to share their first dance. "It's more amazing than I could have dreamed."

"I'm glad it makes you happy. Now, let's see that first dance Mr. and Mrs. Bell."

The dance brought Amy to tears yet again, but they dried up quickly, and the fun began when everyone joined on the dance floor. Wes shared a dance with Amy while Sarah opted for a glass of champagne.

From behind her, she felt someone grab her hand. "May I have this dance?" Before she could turn around and protest, Travis gracefully swung her onto the dance floor. He placed his hand on the small of her back and linked his fingers through hers.

"I guess it wasn't really a question, was it?" Sarah said in response.

Ignoring her, he pushed a curl out of her face before he spun her, "You look stunning. It's enough to take my breath away." When she simply smiled and looked away, he moved his hand lower down on her back. Feeling her body clench, he smiled at her, "So, that's what gets your attention. You don't want compliments, you want action," he said.

"You have no idea what I want," she responded while trying to pull away from him.

Sensing her move, he held on tightly and turned her in to spin, keeping her from escaping. "Oh, I have a feeling it's very similar to what I want, Lieutenant." He stared deeply into her eyes until she turned away.

Before he could say anything else, Wes came up beside them. "May I cut in?" he asked.

"Of course," Travis said, letting go of Sarah's hand and bowing at her. "Thank you for the dance, Lieutenant." Travis turned and headed towards the newlyweds to offer his congratulations.

"I really don't like that guy," Wes said as he twirled her around the dance floor.

"He is just arrogant. I think he likes it when people find him irritating. It's a game to him, to see how fast he can piss someone off. That's all," she said, then kissed him lovingly to comfort his concerns.

"I guess so. I just don't like how much attention he gives you. It seems like he tries extra hard to get you going."

"You are the only one that gets me going, Wesley Porter." She kissed him again, and added a little grab on his butt for good measure. "What you did for Amy just blows me away, Wes."

"Well, I am not done yet. I am going to tell her about our other little surprise."

She had no idea what he was talking about, but just smiled and nodded. She was sure they talked about it before, or else he wouldn't have called it *their* surprise. But, she just couldn't remember what it might be. She figured she was about to find out, since Wes gathered everyone together for a toast. He was so handsome, she thought. His striking blue eyes shined brightly with his smiles as he tapped his champagne glass to get everyone's attention.

"I would like to first say, congratulations to the newlyweds. May your life be filled with happiness and joyful memories," he said as he smiled and saluted Aaron and Amy. "Sarah and I would love it if you guys would start some of those memories with us this weekend, at my place in the Hamptons."

"Are you freaking serious? Sarah, is he serious?" Amy asked with excitement.

Sarah slightly remembered the conversation about a vacation, and how it would be a nice idea as a honeymoon gift. She didn't realize he meant the upcoming weekend, but she went along with him. "Of course he is serious. We couldn't find a toaster in time as a gift, so we thought this would be more practical," Sarah replied.

Amy ran up to them and swung her arms around them simultaneously. "This is so freaking awesome. Oh my God, thank you, thank you, thank you," she gushed as she ran back to Aaron and jumped into his arms. She happily kissed him, "Our first vacation together, and we get to go to the Hamptons!"

Sarah was smiling as she watched her friends. Everyone was smiling as they watched Amy and Aaron's excitement flowing. However, when Sarah's gaze fell on Travis, he sent her a wild grin and rolled his eyes at her. Sarah ignored him and stroked Wes' back with her hand before giving him an affectionate kiss on the check.

When she looked over again, Travis was gone. She felt a twinge of guilt when she realized she was disappointed that he was no longer standing there. She swallowed the feeling and carried on with the night.

Sarah watched Aaron and Amy shove cake into each other's faces at the cake-cutting ceremony. The cake was a red velvet cake flavor, but it was blue and white. The newlyweds were both covered from forehead to chin with blue and white frosting, and happily posed for pictures. As the night went on, one by one, the guests slowly started to head home. Sarah sat beside Wes on one of the plush white couches adorned with blue accent pillows. She put her feet up on his legs and leaned back.

He slipped her heels off and rubbed her feet. "Oh my, you are a God," she said, closing her eyes and enjoying his touch on her throbbing feet. "I don't know the last time I wore heels for that long."

"You looked beautiful," he replied, still rubbing her feet. "I have to say, I am pooped though. It's been a long day."

Aaron and Amy finished saying goodbye to the rest of their guests, and joined Sarah and Wes on the couch across from them.

"This was an amazing night you guys. One for the record books." Amy finished her glass of champagne and continued, "Thank you so much for everything. And for the Hamptons. I am so excited."

"We leave in the morning, so try to get some sleep tonight, even though I know that's the last thing on your minds," Wes winked at them.

"I am going to get my bride home before she passes out on me," Aaron said in response to Amy's big yawn. "Can I help with anything before we go?" Amy asked.

"No you can not," Wes replied. "It will all be taken care of. See you in the morning. Congrats again."

Wes and Sarah hugged them goodbye and headed upstairs. They were both too exhausted for any fun bed games, so they undressed and fell into bed together. Wes wrapped his arms around Sarah. "I love you," he whispered into her ear as they fell asleep together.

Amy and Aaron enjoyed the limo ride home that Wes had arranged. They snuggled in the backseat, sharing one last toast to the night. When they arrived at Aaron's house, he stopped her before she walked through the door. He picked her up and carried her over the threshold. They both giggled and locked lips in a kiss.

When he put her down, she threw her arms around him and kissed him so passionately he could feel the heat radiating off of her body. It stirred his insides and

206

had him wanting much more. As his hands started to roam up and down her body, she pulled away. "I am going to go to the bathroom."

A little flustered and extremely turned on, he took his jacket off and sat on the couch. "Okay," he replied.

When she came back out from the bathroom, the look on his face said it all. She was wearing a very see-through bra and thong lace set. She wore very high matching white lace, stiletto heels. Her toned body was perfectly bronzed and her hard nipples were exposed through the lace material. He could feel his blood pumping through his whole body and his mind became fuzzy with desire for her.

"Hello there, Mr. Bell," she said in a sultry tone as she sauntered towards him.

"Well, hello back, Mrs. Bell," he replied, sitting up on the couch.

She sauntered up and stood before him. He began to run his fingers on top of the soft lavender lace that lightly covered her perky breasts and hard nipples. She leaned in and began unbuttoning his shirt as she knelt down in front of him, planting soft kisses on his neck and chest. She could feel him growing harder by the second, and began to caress him up and down, above his pants. Needing to be released, he unzipped his pants, exposing how erect he was. She took him in her hands and pleasured him until he couldn't stand it any longer.

She stood up and flashed him a naughty smile as she slowly removed her lace top and thong, exposing her perfectly toned physique. He, in turn, removed his shirt. They were now completely naked, flesh-to-flesh, as his fingers found their way up her thigh and quickly entered deep inside her. She moaned out with passion, feeling the hot air escape her lips as she pushed down against his fingers, grinding harder as she begged for more.

He lay down on the couch, pulling her on top of him. She straddled him as she gently slid herself down onto him and began to move back and forth. Her soft red hair fell around her face as she leaned down to kiss him. They almost got lost in a long, passionate kiss as they continued to make love.

Aaron cupped her butt as he pulled her faster, up and down on top of him. Amy's thighs trembled and her breasts shook with each plunge she took down onto him. Aaron's head spun with pleasure with each stroke that brought him closer and closer to climax. She moaned out loudly as he clenched tighter onto her ass. Without thinking about it, she bit into the muscles in his shoulder as her lower body followed suit and clenched down onto him from her intense climax.

Aaron gave one last thrust into her as she cried out with ecstasy, and he then followed her in climax. Afterward, they lay silently, panting, filling the air with their hot breath. Holding hands as beads of sweat enveloped their bodies, they felt the deep love shared between them.

Chapter 30

The sun was beaming through the windows when Sarah awoke. She could smell the fresh coffee and knew Wes had awoken before her. Driven to open her eyes to the scent, she sat up in bed. Wes was at the window with his coffee, staring at the sunrise. When he turned to smile at her, the sun set his eyes on fire and she felt her heart clench. She couldn't believe after all this time, what his smile could still do to her. One look could completely melt her insides.

"Good morning, beautiful," he said, pouring her a cup of coffee. "Ready for a much needed vacation?"

Rubbing her eyes and combing her fingers through her hair, she tried to adjust to the morning light. "I will be after a gallon of coffee," she replied, taking the cup he offered her.

"Well, I let you sleep in a while. The car bringing Amy and Aaron over will be here in twenty minutes."

"Yeah, yeah," she mumbled as she drank her coffee.

Wes walked across the room and into the bathroom. Sarah could hear the shower turn on and see the steam rolling out. "Better get that cute butt of yours going," he hollered from the bathroom. She made her way to the bathroom, setting her cup of coffee on the ledge while she let the water pour down her back. She looked up to see Wes watching her. "I know that look. If you want me ready in twenty minutes, get those thoughts out of your head and get out of here," she said, playfully flicking water at him.

"If I didn't have a car waiting to take us, you would be in trouble," he said, flushing the toilet on his way out.

Sarah screeched and jumped back as the water turned freezing cold. "You jerk!" she screamed after him, knowing he was smiling.

Right on time, twenty minutes later, all four of them were in the car and heading to the Hamptons.

"You two look a little tired this morning," Sarah pointed out. "Did you guys get much sleep?"

Amy and Aaron looked at each other and laughed. "We got some sleep. Enough for a wedding night," Amy replied, kissing Aaron's cheek.

"Walking around in heels all night really does it to me." Sarah continued, "Whenever I do, I sleep like a baby."

"She snores too," Wes added in. Responding to Sarah's appalled face, Wes pinched her side and kissed her hand.

The drive wasn't too long, but long enough to have good conversation and take in the beautiful view. The sun was out and there wasn't a cloud in the sky. As they approached the house that Wes' family owned, the ocean came closer and closer into view. The water was crystal blue and clear enough to see the bottom. The house was on the sand, and two steps off the driveway was the beach.

Amy stepped out of the car and gawked. With her mouth wide open and eyes huge, she could only breathe out, "Wow."

"I always forget you have never been here, Amy," Wes said as he grabbed some of the luggage. "I don't get up here as much as I would like. I think this might actually only be Sarah's fifth or sixth time, right babe?"

"Something like that," she replied, looking around. She had forgotten how truly beautiful and peaceful it was. There was a slight breeze blowing in her hair and the waves were only about one hundred feet away, crashing into the shore. "It's been awhile since I have been up here." She continued, "I almost forgot how stunning it is."

The house was white with blue paneling all around. It was smaller than Wes' house in New York, but much bigger than Sarah's. The front was made up of large windows that looked out to the ocean.

They followed Wes to the door and carried the luggage in after he unlocked it. They walked inside, where the house was white and decorated in a classy beach theme. Picture of sailboats and lighthouses hung on the walls. The ceiling fans were made of wicker, and the blades were leaf-shaped. The furniture was blue and white to the match the outside of the house. The curtains flowed as the breeze came in the front door.

"There are three bedrooms downstairs. They all have some view of the ocean. There are also four bedrooms upstairs. Sarah and I stay upstairs. You can pick any of the other rooms," Wes offered to Amy and Aaron as he set his bags down. "Go ahead and look around before you pick. I will get things settled in and get some food out. I had the fridge and pantry stocked before we came up, and I am starving."

"No complaints here," Amy said, pulling Aaron down the hallway to check out the rooms.

"I think my partner is in heaven," Sarah said, wrapping her arms around Wes. "I don't think I have seen her without a smile in the last couple of days. Her happiness is almost nauseating."

"You are quite the romantic, my dear," he joked, grabbing her butt and kissing her forehead. "Let's get these bags upstairs and get settled. I am ready for some relaxation."

They all met up in the kitchen after they changed into their beachwear. Amy was in a yellow two-piece swimsuit with a matching sheer cover up. She had her red hair pulled back into a long ponytail and big white sunglasses on. Her feet were bare and she had a huge smile, accepting the beer Wes offered her.

Aaron was in black swim trunks and a light black and white zip-up jacket. He wore black flip-flops and black sunglasses. Sarah was surprised to see him so casual. He looked so comfortable and ready for fun. She hadn't pictured him like that before, but she enjoyed watching him sip the beer Wes handed him. Everyone looked so content, and it was just the first day.

Wes leaned back against the counter, drinking his beer when he winked at Sarah. He was in his favorite pair of swim trunks. He called them his Hampton shorts. They were white with blue waves crashing along the sides. They fit the scene perfectly. He had a white button up shirt on that he had left open, showing off his perfectly toned chest. Sarah loved seeing him out of a suit and wondered when the man had time to get such a perfect tan and work on his amazing body.

Wes grabbed her hand as they made their way to the patio. Her long white tube top dress swayed across the top of her bare feet as she walked with him. The patio was large and completely white. There was a fire pit in the middle of a large outdoor couch and several chairs. The fire pit was set up in the middle of a sand pit that resembled being on the beach. The umbrella over the furniture was up and spinning mildly in the breeze.

Sarah clipped her hair back as the breeze blew it around her face. Wes caught a couple of the strays and tucked them behind her ears as they sat.

"What a beautiful day," Aaron said as he sat beside Amy. He linked his fingers with Amy and continued, "We couldn't have asked for a better honeymoon. It's great to be able to spend it with friends." He lifted his beer in salute, "Thanks again."

They all clinked their bottles together and sat around snacking on the chips Wes had brought out.

Amy and Aaron opted to go for a walk and Wes decided it would be a good time to get the grill going. "I got some prime cuts guys. And I happen to be a self-proclaimed grill master," he laughed out. "When you guys get back, we are going to have a killer dinner.

Once Aaron and Amy left on their walk, Sarah made her way to the kitchen where Wes was preparing to cook. "You know, I love it when you get your hands dirty in the kitchen," she said, propping herself up on the kitchen counter to sit.

"You better behave. Don't try to distract me. You don't come between a man and his steak."

Putting her hands up in surrender she said, "Oh, are those the rules? I see. Well, let me know if you need help with anything."

"I am going to cook this meal all by myself and try not to screw it up," he added. "You have a lot going on with your cases. I know you are exhausted. Go relax, babe." He leaned over and pulled her chin down so her lips met his. "Go enjoy the break and ignore the shouting and cursing that may come from here. You only need to get up if you smell smoke."

"That's almost reassuring me on your abilities in the kitchen." She blew him a kiss and laid down on the patio couch, letting the sound of the waves put her to sleep.

She was awakened by the sound of laughter and the smell of amazing food. When she got up, she saw that Amy and Aaron had returned and were helping set the outside table. Inside, Wes had outdone himself. There was a large pile of steaks, corn on the cob, baked beans, mashed potatoes, and rolls of French bread. Sarah was definitely proud. It looked amazing, and smelled even better.

They sat, talked, and ate as the sun began to set. They all complimented Wes on a job well done and complained afterward that they had eaten too much.

"I feel like I might explode," Amy exclaimed while rubbing her belly.

"It's a beautiful sunset, let's walk it off." Wes stood up and reached out to help Sarah up, "Let's take our beers to the beach and watch the sunset."

Aaron chased Amy down to the sand and playfully tackled her. Once on the ground, she found a spot in his lap to sit and cuddle. He put his arms around her waist and kissed the back of her neck.

Wes and Sarah sat in the sand next to one another. She leaned against him as they held hands and watched the sun disappear behind the ocean. Before the sky went dark, it was streaked with orange, pink, red, and purple tones. The sky had looked like a painting on a canvas. Breathtaking was not a word enough to capture it.

The darkness of night had overtaken the house and Wes was forced to turn the patio lights on. The lights overtook the stars in the sky, but he needed them to see and set up the game.

Sarah did not love games, but she agreed to play to appease Wes and her friends. They had all settled on a couple's trivia game. Surprisingly, after just ten minutes, Sarah was laughing and having as much fun playing the game as everyone else. They played several rounds before taking a break for more beer and snacks. As the night continued, they played, snacked, and drank until the early morning hours. Sarah was happy, and couldn't remember the last time she had so much fun.

Chapter 31

Sex was the farthest thing from her mind tonight, but she needed the money, as usual. She had chosen her signature black mini skirt with a skintight blue snake print top. She was five inches taller tonight due to her killer black stilettos. Her blonde wig was pulled back into pigtails with blue ribbons holding them in place. She had sprayed her favorite perfume on before walking out the door. Three long necklaces draped around her chest and large silver hoops adorned her ears. She knew she would be hard to miss tonight.

The last thing she felt like doing was smiling, but she plastered one on at every guy that walked by. It was a shame these Johns paid her bills. She despised most of them. It was rare to get a decent guy as a client, and impossible to have one that respected her at all. She was just doing what she had to do. After all, who were they to judge? She had to pay her bills and not everybody had more than one skill set. She knew she didn't. She had just the one and it happened to be sex. So, she exploited that skill set and made her money, night after night.

"Hey sugar," she said, winking at a man strolling by. He took the time to look her up and down, but didn't stop long enough to show interest. She kept walking and had to plaster her fake smile on for the next guy. He was a tall man around forty years old. He was leaning against the wall of a small convenience store, smoking a cigarette. She really hated cigarettes, and smelling of them. But, his look lingered on her long enough for her to know he was more than interested.

"Hey baby. You looking for a good time tonight?" she said, leaning with one hand against the wall next to him and the other on her hip as she stuck her long, lean leg out.

He flicked his cigarette into the street and ran his fingers through one of her pigtails. "As a matter of fact, I am. I have a room too, around the corner."

"Perfect. Looks like it's your lucky night, sugar." She let him take the lead and head to the room, which turned out to be in a shabby motel. It had been wishful thinking to assume it might be a room in a semi-decent hotel.

The name of the motel wasn't even legible since four out of the seven letters in its nameplate had burnt out. It was a small, single story place, and probably no more than twenty rooms. From the look on the manager's face of boredom, she assumed most of the rooms were vacant. As scummy as the place was, being hassled by him wasn't something she wanted to deal with. The door to room number three was opened, and the scent of stale smoke overwhelmed her. The only thing going through her mind was hoping this guy didn't like to kiss. It was one thing to fake a smile and an orgasm, but it might be hard to not vomit in his mouth if that's what he tasted like.

The room was small and confining. A king bed took up the wall where the bathroom door was, with a small nightstand next to it. On the opposite wall was a small television on a stand. She laughed when she noticed the small placard on the stand that said, "Thank you for not smoking."

There was a small sofa chair, the color of pumpkin orange, against the last wall with a small round table next to it. To add to the ugly décor, the bed comforter was the same color, with obnoxiously bright orange pillows. The carpet was a dull brown and she wondered if it had originally been that color, or had dinged from age. Either way, she probably didn't care to know.

He closed the door behind her and they discussed what he wanted, and what the price would be. Once the discussion was over, he moved to the bed, stripping from the waist down. He sat there with a smile and a flaccid, limp dick in his hand. Apparently, she was really going to have to work for her money tonight.

She knelt down in front of him, and took his lifeless member in her mouth. She moved it around, using her tongue to stimulate his blood flow. She could feel him growing with each tongue flip. As she continued to arouse him with her mouth, his hands found their way under her shirt. He rubbed his rough hand over her breasts while the other pulled on her pigtail. He used his fingers to flick at her breasts and it took all of her self-control not to smack him. She had to keep reminding herself that rent was still due.

When he was ready, he pulled her head back by her hair and asked her to get undressed. She slowly slipped her shirt over her head and slid the skirt off, down her long legs. She opted to wear no panties tonight, which left her standing in front of him in her bra and heels. He stood to unhook her bra for her and whispered in her ear, "Keep the heels on."

He motioned her onto the bed and climbed above her. He slowly slid himself inside her and she started on her scene. Well, that's what she called it, having sex with the Johns. She imagined she was doing a show and acted her way through it. He held himself up on his arms and thrust in and out of her. She moaned and arched her back to show him how much she was enjoying it.

218

Feeling uncomfortable with him staring at her, she closed her eyes. That's when she felt his hands around her throat.

Her eyes shot open and she started kicking and squirming. "I will put you in your place, whore," he screamed, and spit flew out of his mouth. "You think you can keep killing men and get away with it? I will show you we are superior, bitch, and I will be called a hero. The people of New York will thank me for turning you in." He kept screaming at her with his hands getting tighter and tighter around her throat.

She could feel her chest burning as she fought for air. Her body was pinned by his, and she could not get out from under him. As her arms were flailing, her hand landed on something hard and she used all her strength to pick it up. Before she even realized it, it was an alarm clock she was hitting him in the head with. He let go of her throat to wipe at the blood dripping down his face, "You bitch," he shouted.

She used the free breath she had, to scream. She wiggled out from underneath him and was heading for the door when the manager opened it. "Oh, thank you, please help me," she said, happy to see him.

From behind her, the man was getting dressed and yelling. "This woman attacked me. She is the prostitute they have been talking about on the news. Call the police. Call the police."

She stood there, dumbfounded as the man took a cell phone from his pocket and dialed 9-1-1. There was a ringing in her ears, and a fuzziness in her head as she tried to comprehend what was going on. The manager was telling the police that she attacked a man and was responsible for a bunch of murders. Her hands were now being held behind her back by the John and she started to sob, waiting for the police to show up.

Chapter 32

It was almost three in the morning and Wes, Sarah, Amy, and Aaron were still up playing the trivia game. Sarah stopped giggling when her phone rang. There was only one reason why her phone would ring at three in the morning. That reason was death.

Everyone stopped laughing and stared at her while she answered the phone. She picked up and listened intently. The look on her face was of surprise. She continued to listen intently, and nodded. When she hung up on the phone, she was quiet for a moment.

"What is it babe?" Wes asked, walking over to her. He rubbed his hand down her back, waiting for an answer.

"That was Travis. I mean, Special Agent Stone," she corrected. "He said they have a suspect in custody for the case."

"The Sex Slayer case?" Amy questioned, with much excitement.

Sarah crossed her arms over her chest and continued. "It would seem so. Apparently a hotel manager had to use his key to open a room when he heard yelling and fighting. Hearing about the killings on the news, he wanted to make sure nothing bad was going on. He said the woman was naked and the guy was bleeding from the head and shouting that she was trying to kill him. He said she was the one who attacked all of the other men. Police took her into custody when they arrived, and she is being held for questioning. Agent Stone was informed, and he called me, figuring I would want to conduct the interview with him."

"Wow, that's great, Sarah. I know how much you would love to close this case."

"It's not that easy, Wes." Sarah walked over and sat down on the couch. "If I don't get a confession out of her, it's going to take a serious amount of work to put her in each place, with each guy. Our girl was more than careful about leaving nothing behind here. Even having her in custody, it will prove very difficult to close this without a confession."

"If anyone can pull a confession out of someone, it's definitely you babe," Wes said, sitting next to her on the arm of the couch.

"I'm so sorry guys, but I have to go," she said, standing up. "They want to do the interview as soon as they can, and if I am not there, I know Agent Stone will conduct it without me. There's no way in hell I am letting that happen."

Amy stood up too," I will get packed and head out with you, Lieutenant."

"That's not necessary. Enjoy your wedding weekend. It is just an interview. I promise, if anything comes up that you need to be a part of, I will make you get your ass back to town. But, for now, enjoy your time off. That's an order, Detective," she said, smiling at Amy. She kissed Wes on the cheek and headed upstairs to pack.

Wes followed her upstairs and watched her as she packed, "You've had a little bit to drink, will you be fine to drive?"

"Shit, no, I shouldn't be driving yet, after the drinks I've had.

"That's what I thought. It's fine babe, I've already called for a car. It should be here in a few minutes," Wes said.

"Thank you," Sarah replied. She heaved her bag over her shoulder and walked to Wes. She grabbed his hand and kissed him. "I'm sorry our weekend got interrupted. You know I wouldn't go if it was not important," she told him.

Wes walked Sarah to the front door, where they said their goodbyes.

"Keep me in the loop, please," Amy requested. "I want to know when you break her."

"Of course. Enjoy your honeymoon. If I can head back up, I will."

Wes walked her out to the car in the driveway. "Call me when you get there, babe." He reached up and framed her face in his hands before pressing his lips to hers in a passionate kiss. "Love you babe."

"I love you too. I'm sorry I have to go. But, go inside and have fun with them. You don't get a vacation very often," she said as she got in the car.

Chapter 33

The driver dropped Sarah off at the station at five in the morning. She was exhausted, but she knew she wanted to be a part of this interview.

She ran straight into Travis when she got off the elevator. "You know, Lieutenant, you have had a bad habit of running into me and ruining my clothes," he said, wiping at the new coffee stain on his white shirt.

"Well, if you weren't under my feet or in my face all the time, that wouldn't happen," she snapped back as she pushed away from him, towards her office.

He followed her, "Well, aren't we just a ball of sunshine on this fine morning?" He set the coffee down on her desk, and smiled when she stared at it. "Yes, Lieutenant, that coffee is for you. Here, I am, trying to be nice, and you are mean to me. Don't you feel bad now?" he smirked.

She picked up the cup and took a long swallow, "Not at all, Agent Stone." She picked up her files and walked out of her office, down the hall. Knowing he was right behind her, she asked him to fill her in. "I need all the details before I go in there. Which interview room?"

Travis filled her in on what he knew, as they walked. "The arresting officers said she was in tears the whole way here and saying this guy attacked her."

"The one that she was picked up with?" At his nod, she continued, "So, she is naked when the manager busts in, he is bleeding from the head, and they are both

224

accusing each other of attacking the other one. Got it. What's her name?"

"Diamond," he replied with a smile.

Sneering at him, Sarah stopped at the interview room door. "Her real name is what, Ace."

"I get nicknames. Now, I like that," he said, putting his hands in his pocket and rolling back on his heels. At her eye rolling he answered her question, "her legal name is Diamond. She had it changed three years ago, from Stephanie Smith."

"I can see why a street girl would want a sexier name than Stephanie Smith. It doesn't exactly scream sex goddess; maybe girl next door, which is exactly what she looks like," Sarah said, staring through the one-way window. It was hard to tell age past the puffy and swollen eyes beneath the tears, but she looked young. Her hair was light brown and cut short to fall beneath her ears. She was in grey sweats and a grey sweatshirt, compliments of the NYPD, and black flip-flops. She sat with her cuffed hands in her lap, and a sullen look on her face.

"That's not what she looked like when she was picked up. She was done up and fit the name Diamond, more than the name Stephanie." As he reached for the handle on the door, Sarah stopped him as she slapped her files against his chest.

"I am doing this alone," she stated, and stepped past him, blocking his way to the door.

"Like hell you are," he quickly replied.

Sarah laid a hand on his chest and smiled sweetly up at him. "If this is our girl, she kills men. You are a man. If this isn't our girl, this is a young woman who just went through a traumatizing experience with a man.

225

Again, you are a man. She is not going to be comfortable with you in there. I go in alone. You can observe, and I will put an earpiece in, so I can hear you."

He grabbed the hand she still had on his chest before she could pull it away, and winked at her. "Only because you asked so nicely," he smirked.

Sarah pulled her hand away and risked one last look at Travis before she closed the interview room door. She walked in and sat across form the young woman known as Diamond. She didn't resemble a diamond right now. There was no sparkle, no shine, no hardness. She was pale, looked tired, and her eyes were pleading for someone to help her. She looked as far from a man-killer as they came.

"Good morning, Diamond. I am Lieutenant Sarah Carmichael. I understand you have waived your rights to have council present. Is that correct?"

Before the words came out, the girl was sobbing again. In between sniffles, she answered, "I didn't do anything wrong, why do I need a lawyer?"

"Anytime you are brought into police custody, and to undergo questioning, you have a right to have council. Would you like to request council at this time Stephanie? Can I call you Stephanie?"

She shook her head and pity filled Sarah's stomach as tears continued to stream down her face. "No one has called me that in a long time, but I guess you can. And I don't want to wait for council. I want to get this over with and go home. I didn't do anything wrong. That man is telling people I killed someone. I could never kill anyone. Why is he saying that? He is the one who tried to hurt me."

"Just take a minute to calm down and we will continue. Just tell me about tonight, and from there we will work on the other nights in question." Sarah waited for the woman to take a few breaths before continuing, "Walk me through your whole day. Start from waking up this morning until you got here with me."

Stephanie took a deep breath and went through her whole day. She included everything she had eaten and everyone she came in contact with. She gave every detail of her day, and seemed to be telling the truth. She only got uneasy when she spoke about the motel room. "I know prostitution is illegal and you can arrest me for that, but that's all I did. He paid me for sex, and I let him have sex with me. Everything was fine and normal until he started strangling me." Her eyes began to overflow with tears again, and her breathing became quick and shallow. "He kept calling me a whore and screaming at me about showing me who was superior. He kept asking who I thought I was by killing all those men and that he would be a hero for turning me in. He is crazy," she screamed. "I have never killed anyone and I have never met that man before tonight."

"Okay. Do the names Adam Wright or Keith Simon mean anything to you?"

"If I said no, I would be lying. But, I don't know them. I only recognize the names because they have been splashed all over the news." Obviously, catching on, her eyes got wide and she paled. "That's what this is about? That guy is saying I am the woman who killed those men? No. No," she responded. "I admit to prostitution and disliking most of the guys I have to sleep with, but I have never hurt any of them. That's just not who I am."

Sarah questioned her for an hour about all the nights in question, and the other people involved. Stephanie gave alibis for the recent events, but had a hard time remembering where she had been during the first murders. Sarah could tell the girl was exhausted, and felt her own overwhelming exhaustion kicking in. "I will tell you what, Stephanie. I am going to have my officers check out your alibis while you get some sleep. I know this isn't the ideal place to rest, but we need to get some things squared away. Get some rest, and we will talk again later today, when maybe your mind has cleared some and you can remember more information for me."

Stephanie put her head in her hands and rubbed her eyes. "Okay," she replied. As Sarah got up to walk out, Stephanie stopped her with a whisper, "I didn't do this, Lieutenant."

"If that's the case, I will get you out of here as soon as possible. I like to close cases, but I will not put an innocent person away to do that. You have my word on that," she said, stepping into the hallway. This time, she stopped short to avoid running into Travis.

"So, what do you think Lieutenant?" he asked, following her.

"I am not sure she's our girl. My gut it telling me she doesn't have it in her."

"Maybe your gut is as exhausted as you are. This is hard for me to say, but you look like shit, doll." He pushed her through her office door and sat her down in her chair.

"Don't call me dol–," she began, but was cut off when he started rubbing her shoulders. His hands were powerful and they made her skin feel like jelly. She was tense and the massaging hurt, but it was a blissful kind of pain. Before she realized it, she was sinking into her seat and moaning. "Oh, yeah, oh my God, that feels so good."

Travis stood behind her smiling, his mind racing with thoughts of having his hands all over her body. "Yeah, I am pretty damn good with my hands. They can work wonders all over your body."

Realizing the situation, Sarah shot out of her chair. "I'm going to find a bunk to put my feet up. I haven't been to sleep yet, but don't let me sleep for more than two hours." She walked past him and avoided all contact. On her way out, without turning to him she said, "Thanks for the shoulder rub. It helped with the tension.

He watched her leave, enjoying the way her tight jeans squeezed her butt. Tension was the only thing he could think about. He felt it every time he was with her. They both wanted to touch each other, and she kept fighting it and denying it. She was the cause of the tension. Standing in her office with her scent still lingering, he felt his arousal grow, as well as his need for her. He was done denying what he wanted. He was going to make her stop denying. He knew she wanted him, and he was going to have her.

With desire and determination, he left her office and headed to the loft. The loft was a small room with no windows and four cots, but the officers liked to joke and call it the loft. Travis pictured her in that room, on her back, hopefully waiting for him.

When he opened the door, her eyes shot open. "What the fuck. I told you I needed some rest." She knew, by the look on his face, what he meant when he locked the door behind him.

She started to speak as she attempted to swing her legs off the cot and get up, but he stopped her. "Just shut up, Sarah," he stopped her as he knelt before her, wrapped his hands in her hair, and devoured her mouth with his. The heat was instant and he could hear his ears ringing. He had a mix of excitement and fear, unsure if she would smack him. But, she kissed him back.

She ran her hand through his hair as they continued to taste each other. He then put his hand on her waist as he guided her down onto the cot and laid her on her back. He was above her, now running his fingers all over her trembling body. His hands were wild, but he couldn't think of anything else he wanted more than to rub them all over every inch of her body.

He broke away from the kiss to unbutton her shirt and their eyes met. He was afraid when the kiss was over that she would panic and try to deny him again, but instead, she stared intently right back at him. She moved her fingers down her shirt and unbuttoned it for him, exposing her soft breast beneath a lace bra.

Travis now grew bold and moved his hands down to the clasp on her belt. He slowly slid it off while unbuttoning her pants, catching a glimpse of her soft cotton white panties below. He felt himself grow increasingly larger as he undid the clasp on the back of her bra, dropping it to the floor. Sarah lifted her ass up, just enough for him to slide her pants and panties off. She now lay there, fully exposed to him, shaking from anticipation and excitement.

Travis removed his clothes as he stood above her, keeping his eyes fixated on her sensual naked body as he climbed on top of her. The warmth of her body felt good against him in the cool of the room. Sarah was powerless against the soft kisses he planted on her neck. She squirmed and moaned as he ran his tongue just under her ear, then down the side of her neck to her shoulder. He brandished her with little nips and sucks that made her pull him in harder against her as she felt his hard sex throb against her thigh. He groaned as her hand made its way down to his member as she gently gripped it in her fingers, slowly stroking it back and forth.

Their lips met again in a hot, wet kiss. Sarah knew what she was doing was wrong, but she was intoxicated by him and unable to stop. She continued to stroke him before finally spreading her legs and guiding him inside of her. He grunted as he began pounding into her with slow, hard thrusts, nearly picking her up each time. The friction between them felt excruciatingly good. She pushed herself into him with every thrust he made, adjusting her hips to the perfect angle to take him in each time. She felt him deeper and deeper with every glide he offered into her.

He moved faster and faster, as she felt her orgasm rushing out like lightning from between her legs. Travis watched her squirm as he hungrily grabbed a cup full of her breast and took it into his mouth as he took his last stroke inside of her before climaxing.

They laid there, breathing each other's scent in, before Sarah's mixture of panic and guilt bore down on her. She shoved Travis off of her and quickly dressed. He sat watching her, and knew what was going through her mind.

"Don't do this, Sarah. There is nothing wrong with what we feel for each other." He reached over and tried to grab her hand, but she pulled it away quickly.

"Don't," she said, as she finished buttoning her shirt. She buckled her belt and looked straight into his eyes, "This was a mistake and it will never happen again."

Travis dressed as quickly as she had, and tried to stop her from opening the door. He put his body weight against it as he put his shirt on. "Let's just talk about it. Please don't run out."

"There is nothing to talk about. I don't cheat. I am not the kind of person that would ever hurt Wes like this. I don't know what the fuck just happened. I am going to blame it on exhaustion and deal with it myself. Now, move," she snapped, pulling the door open hard enough to make him fumble forward.

He sat down on the cot, completely defeated, as the door closed. He knew her guilt would kick in, but he had hoped to share more intimate time with her before it did. He hoped they could work through what she was feeling. He wanted what they just shared to be enough. But, he knew it wasn't.

Sarah walked quickly to the elevator. It took everything inside of her to keep from running. But, she didn't want to make a scene. She didn't want to alert anybody that there was something wrong, but she needed out. She rode the elevator up to the top floor, fighting to not crawl out of her skin. Her mind was racing and her body was numb, remembering all the places he had just touched her. She sucked in a breath of fresh air, exiting the elevator as she burst into tears.

"What have I done?" she asked herself. "How could I do this to Wes?" She cried harder as she thought of how she left him in the Hamptons, and left the beautiful vacation he planned for them. Instead, she had betrayed him. She betrayed his trust and his love. She sat against the wall with her head in her lap and her arms wrapped around her body. She let the waves of tears and anger and guilt wash through her. Sitting with her head still in her lap, her phone rang. She cursed to herself.

Looking at the caller ID, she cursed out loud. "Fuck Wes, perfect timing." She wasn't sure if she should answer the phone or not. Not wanting to worry him, she collected herself, took a breath, and answered, "Hello."

"Hey there, beautiful," he said from the other end. "I know you are busy, so I will keep it short. But, I wanted to see how you were feeling. I know you are working on no sleep right now."

She could feel her heart ripping her stomach to shreds and she fought to not be sick. She loved his voice and now the sound of it was making her dizzy and nauseous, knowing what she had just done. "I am tired, but making it," she lied. "If the day calls for it, I will cut out early and go home."

"Okay, babe. Don't work too hard." He said something to Aaron in the background, and she could hear laughing. "Sorry, Aaron is attempting to show Amy how to, what did he just call it, drop it like it's hot. It's quite amusing. Anyway, I am going to head back tomorrow and let them have some time here alone. Maybe you and I can have a little alone time too, if the case permits."

"Okay," was all she could manage to say as she repeatedly mentally slapped herself.

"I can tell you are busy and I don't want to keep you. Love you babe."

"I love you too Wes." Once the conversation was over, she sat, staring at the phone. "I love you so much, you have no idea," she said to herself. "What have I done?" She repeated the question over and over, aloud, and in her head. This just was not who she was. She was not supposed to be the one who caused others pain. She was not someone who betrayed and hurt the people she loved. She questioned who she had become. She didn't have the answer, and she was beginning to scare herself.

She saw what cheating and lying did to people. She had seen the pain and suffering it caused others. She had seen the hurt turn into anger and rage. She had personally seen the devastation it caused some families when she showed up in the aftermath. It didn't always end up with death, but it always ended up with a part of someone dying. She was now going to be responsible for a part of Wes dying, and his heart breaking.

Sarah took twenty minutes in the fresh air and let it cleanse her mind. No matter how she felt and what was going on in her personal life, she had a job to do. She knew this girl, Diamond, didn't kill anyone and she needed to do her job by proving it. No innocent person deserved to be locked up or hurt like that. The nausea came and went as she rode the elevator back down.

When she entered her office, she saw Travis ending a phone call. "Damn it," he muttered after he had hung up. He turned to see her enter, "There you are."

"Look, I can't do this with you right now. I have a case to work on." She sat down behind her desk and tried to ignore him.

"Well, it appears I do as well." He sat down in the chair across from her and raked his fingers through his hair. "Some hikers in Arizona just found a mass grave. There are at least fifteen bodies, and they match the M.O. of a case I worked out there almost three years ago that was never solved. They want me out there tomorrow. I am on the first flight out in the morning."

Sarah felt her tension ease a bit. The best thing that could happen was for him to leave. She had been wishing for it and now he actually was. She took a long, silent breath of relief.

Travis leaned forward with his elbows on her desk. "I will come back. I need to see you again."

Immediately, all of the relief she was feeling, vanished. She needed him to leave and never come back.

It didn't matter what she felt for him, it wouldn't compare to what she felt for Wes, and she needed to protect Wes from getting hurt. She needed Travis out of her life, and she needed Wes to never think about him again.

"From the day I met you, I haven't been able to stop thinking about you. I know you feel the same way. I know you love Wes, but you have feelings for me. We need to talk about this. Wes needs to know so we can all be adults and come to a conclusion. If he can forgive you and still wants to work it out, I will fight for you Sarah. You can say you don't want me, but I know you do and I will fight for you, to see what this can be."

The sickness and tension was back. "Well, having feelings for you and you having feelings for me is a problem and an inconvenience. It's not one that I need or want in my life," she said harshly.

"We are adults, and we can figure this out as such. Just give me a chance. I am due for a conference call in five minutes, but I really think we should talk. We can come up with a solution to this, together."

The feelings she was trying to deny that she had, caused a serious problem for her. She needed a solution. She wrote down her address on a small piece of paper and handed it to him. "Wes is in the Hamptons until tomorrow morning. This is my address. Be there at eight tonight and we can talk. I am all for solutions, and I will find one tonight." She watched him leave and mentally cursed.

She thought about how one instance can change an entire life. One wrong person enters, and the whole path gets turned on its side and her world gets thrown off its axis. One wrong move throws a hitch in plans, and there is no coming back from it. That is one thing Sarah knew for sure. There was no going back now.

Chapter 34

Travis couldn't believe how nervous he felt standing outside Sarah's place. He really hoped they could find a way to make this work. Whatever *this* was, he wanted it to work. He wanted to be with her. He couldn't stop thinking about her and the way her body had felt beneath his hands. He couldn't stop thinking of how she tasted and how she moaned with pleasure for him. He knew he would never be able to forget it or be without it. As much as she denied it, he knew she felt the same way. He could see it in her eyes when he had entered her and made love to her. There was an intense attraction and chemistry there that he refused to overlook or forget.

She sat inside waiting for Travis. She had called Wes and told him that she was turning in for the night. She said she was exhausted and needed to go to bed early to get her mind clear. Her mind was clearer than ever though. The guilt had turned into a need; a need to protect Wes from the pain of what she had done and what she had become. She needed to get a grip on things. It was time to take back control of her life.

He knocked on her door and was treated to a smile when she opened it. He was a little surprised to see her in skintight black leggings and a midriff baring black shirt. She was barefoot and her hair was pulled back into a tight ponytail. He walked in and took a seat when she offered. "Thank you for seeing me. I really needed to be with you again before I have to leave," he said, looking around the room.

He was sitting on a small futon converted to a couch. He could see into the closet as the door was left open. There were clothes of all different colors and numbers of shoes. Most of them were extreme heels. They were nothing like he pictured her wearing. He looked over to the vanity against the wall. It was covered with different types of make-up and he could see wigs hanging from it. There were wigs of all different colors and lengths. She had a long, light brown wig hanging next to a cropped, dark brown one. Below it was a short, black wig. On the other side of the vanity was a platinum blonde wig filled with curls and a fiery red one that stood out in the sparse room.

Travis sat, staring around, confused and baffled. "I thought you had a house?" he asked her as she walked up to sit beside him.

"This is a studio filled with what looks like streetwalker attire. I am really confused."

She sat next to him with her hand on top of his. She kept the smile on her face and looked deep into his eyes. "You said you wanted a solution tonight. I am going to solve the problem."

He linked his fingers in hers and his eyes begged for answers, "What is all this, Sarah?"

She unlinked her fingers from him and placed her hand on his chest. She could feel his heart beating rapidly beneath her fingers. "Tonight, I am solving our problem. Tonight, in this place, you can call me Lucy Lust."

Travis barely had time to comprehend what she ha said before the scalpel she had stolen from the morgue was jabbed into his heart. It was a perfect shot and just a small trickle of blood seeped through his shirt as she watched the life flow from his eyes. It had been fast and painless. He would be dead before he felt any pain or realized what was going on.

Once again, Sarah let Lucy solve her problems for her. When it came to money, Lucy had always helped her out. When she needed escape her reality, Lucy was always there. Travis wanted a solution, and now, Lucy helped Sarah get the solution she wanted. Travis was gone and Wes would never have to know about her indiscretion. Her temptation was gone for good now, and she never had to worry about hurting Wes the way her stepfather had hurt her mother.

"He brought this upon himself, pushing too damn hard" she said out loud. She wasn't sure if she was trying to justify it to herself, the stable, law abiding New York City Police Officer, or to Lucy Lust, the streetwalker who seemed to always find trouble. Ever since Adam Wright had come into her life, things had been out of control. Not anymore, she thought.

She looked over at Travis before getting up. She would deal with him tomorrow. She strolled out and locked the door to the studio. Sarah was going home. Lucy would clean up the mess when she was back on the clock. Tonight, it was time to go home, to her real home; to her real bed, for some real sleep.

Her world could be put back in place now and she could work on getting control over it again. Problem solved, she thought, smiling and walking down the street as she dialed Wes on the phone.

Problem solved.

End

239